W9-BRU-858

LOVERS IN PARADISE

The tears ran down Roxana's face as she looked at her carving of Viktor. She would rather die than live without his love.

To perfect her art and protect her secret Roxana had stayed on in Bali after the mysterious death of her uncle, enduring the harsh rule of the Dutch and the attentions of a debauched Governor.

When the cynical Count Viktor van Haan arrived from Holland it seemed as though the island's ancient gods drew them together. Roxana trembled with the wonder of his kisses until fate intervened and he had turned from her in disgust.

Would Viktor ever believe her innocence and seek her out amid the awesome beauty of the mountains to hold her fast until their souls and their bodies were one.

Other Barbara Cartland titles
in Large Print

No Darkness for Love
A Rhapsody of Love
A Fugitive from Love
Escape
Love on the Wind
For all Eternity
Lies for Love
Journey to a Star
Love is an Eagle
Love Casts Out Fear
A Hazard of Hearts
Elizabethan Lover

LOVERS IN PARADISE

Lovers in Paradise

by
Barbara Cartland

MAGNA PRINT BOOKS
Long Preston, North Yorkshire,
England.

British Library Cataloguing in Publication Data.

Cartland, Barbara, *1902—*
  Lovers in paradise.
  I. Title
  823'.912(F)

  ISBN 1-85057-351-4
  ISBN 1-85057-352-2 Pbk

First Published in Great Britain by Pan Books Ltd. 1979

Copyright © 1979 by Cartland Promotions.

Published in Large Print 1989 by arrangement with the Copyright holder.

All rights reserved. No part of this publication may be reproduced, stored in a retrieval system, or transmitted in any form or by any means, electronic, mechanical, photocopying, recording or otherwise, without the prior permission of the Copyright owner.

Printed and bound in Great Britain by
Redwood Burn Limited, Trowbridge, Wiltshire.

Author's Note

On the 27th May 1905 a Chinese steamer was shipwrecked on the beach of Sanur about four miles from Badung. The Balinese looted the wreckage as they had done for centuries, but the Dutch Government claimed an indemnity of 7,500 florins from the Radja of Badung. He considered such a request an insult and refused to pay.

This was the excuse the Dutch were waiting for and in 1906 they sent an expeditionary force into South Bali. Surrounded on all sides by Dutch troops the defenders, seeing their cause was lost, decided to die rather than surrender.

During the night of the 20th September the Prince set fire to the Palace and next morning opened the gates. Thousands of

Balinese advanced slowly towards the Dutch guns. The men sparkling with jewels wore their ceremonial red, black and gold costumes, the women carrying their children wore pure white sarongs and were also covered in jewels and pearls.

On a throne supported by the tallest warriors in the Radja, a slender young man sat, pale and silent. Suddenly within fifty yards of the Dutch the Radja drew his *kris* from its scabbard. This was the signal and the Balinese fell on their swords.

They shared a curious exaltation at the thought of death. They dedicated themselves and the sacrifice of their bodies was but the shadow of reality. It was an offering to the gods in the age-old struggle between good and evil.

The Dutch Captain gave the order to fire and the slaughter began. The Radja fell and so did hundreds of his followers—wounded women stabbed their babies for fear they should survive, then husbands killed their wives. The Balinese warriors and children brandishing spears and knives charged the firing cannon.

Three times the Dutch ceased fire in an attempt to stop the slaughter, but the Balinese had decided to die.

Apart from a few babies there were no survivors of the massacre. This was the end— the Dutch were now the masters of all Bali.

Today the square in Des Pasar, the former Badune where it took place, has become a football-ground.

In 1920 and in 1924 more temporary permits were given to Catholic and Protestant missionaries to carry on the work in Bali, but all their efforts were doomed to failure.

In 1945 the Dutch East Indies established their independence. The Republic was proclaimed five years later and the whole archipelago took the name of Indonesia.

CHAPTER ONE

1892

Count Viktor van Haan looked sullenly at the glistening rice fields, the forest-crowned mountain peaks and the feathery coconut palms shimmering in the sunshine.

Everything was green: the lush green rice fields, the trees, the valleys. Even the frangipani and tjempake blossoms seemed somehow to lose their delicate white beauty in the green which surrounded them.

The Count had thought as he stepped from the steamship which seemed to him to have taken an unconscionable time to reach Bali that exile, however beautiful, was oppressive.

Although it might be perhaps for only a short time, including the months of travel, for less than a year, it was in fact exile in a way undeniably humiliating to his self-esteem.

When the Queen Dowager had sent for him to come to the Palace in Amsterdam he had expected it to be the usual request to attend a Court function or receive on her behalf some distinguished visitor to Holland.

Such requests she had often made to him in the past, knowing that his charm, diplomacy and knowledge of the world were extremely useful when there was no King of the Netherlands to perform such functions.

He told himself however that the Queen Dowager had utilised quite enough of his time in the last few months, and he had no intention of being pressurised into doing anything that was not of particular interest to him.

Too often he had found himself saddled with extremely boring and pompous Statesmen and had found the long drawn-out banquets and interminable conferences almost unendurable.

It was understandable that the Count, who was spoken of as the most attractive man in Holland and was a distant cousin of the Queen Dowager, should be in great demand.

On the death of William III in 1890 Princess Wilhelmina had become Queen at the age of ten.

Her mother had been appointed Queen Regent, and now two years later the little Queen Wilhelmina was, of course, still in the School-Room.

The Count had always been very fond of his cousin and quite prepared to offer her his loyalty and his respect.

Also when it suited him he was willing to wait attendance on her and perform the many duties she required of him so long as they did not come too often into conflict with his own plans.

It was not surprising that by the time he was thirty he had become selfish and very conscious of his own prestige.

He was not only extremely handsome, but he had a personality which impressed all those who visited the dull, conventional Dutch Court.

This was due perhaps to the fact that the Count was himself only half-Dutch.

His father had been head of one of the most respected and honoured families in the whole country.

The history of the van Haans was also the history of the Netherlands, and it was difficult to speak of any great event in which the Dutch had taken part without finding that a van Haan was present.

But the Count's mother had been French, the daughter of the *Duc* de Briac.

She had not only been beautiful but acclaimed for her intelligence and sparkling gaiety, and was *persona grata* in all the intellectual Salons which were patronised in Paris by everyone of consequence.

Everyone predicted that an alliance between Count Hendrih van Haan and Madeleine de Briac was bound to result in their progeny being exceptional.

Their son Viktor had measured up to all

their expectations and now that his father was dead he found himself the owner of possessions to which the only rival was the Crown itself.

As he passed through the over-ornamented rooms of the Palace to the Queen Dowager's apartments he thought, as he had thought so often before, that they needed re-decorating and re-arranging.

There were treasures, especially pictures, of inestimable value, but they were badly displayed.

The Count's good taste was continually irritated by the fact that the Queen Dowager and those who served her were complacently pleased with their surroundings and had no intention of countenancing any change.

A flunkey in the resplendent Royal livery opened the doors of the Queen Dowager's private Drawing-Room and the Count walked in to find, as he had expected, that she was alone.

He bowed conventionally over her hand and was not surprised to see an unmistakable glint of admiration in her eyes.

It was an expression the Count was accustomed to seeing when any woman old or young looked at him, and if it had not been there he would certainly have questioned why it was missing.

The admiration in the Queen Dowager's eyes, was however, quickly replaced by one of anxiety.

'I sent for you, Viktor,' she said in her quiet voice, 'to inform you that something very serious has happened and I wished you to learn of it from me rather than anybody else.'

'What can have occurred?' the Count enquired.

He wondered as he spoke if the Queen Dowager had learnt of a rather regrettable party he had given two nights ago.

He thought while it was taking place that his guests' behaviour would undoubtedly cause a scandal if anybody talked the next day.

But people, even the Dutch, accepted

some looseness of behaviour in those who belonged to the Theatrical world, especially when they were French.

He thought it unlikely that the Queen Dowager should have been told of certain regrettable incidents although one could never be sure who would whisper spitefully in her ear and what tales she would find it expedient to remember.

'What has upset you?' he asked. 'If it concerns me, I can only express my deepest regrets, Ma'am, that you should have been troubled.'

He always addressed the Queen Dowager formally and he knew that she liked the way he did not presume on their relationship.

'I am indeed upset,' she replied, 'and I am afraid, Viktor, you are involved.'

The Count raised his eye-brows and waited.

He was not really apprehensive as to what might be disclosed. He knew only too well how any tit-bit of gossip could be mouthed over and exaggerated in Court Circles, and it was inevitable that he would always be suspected of the worst.

The Queen Dowager drew in a deep breath as if to sustain herself, then she said:

'Luise van Heydberg killed herself last night!'

She spoke without emotion, and yet it seemed as if the monotonous tone of her voice echoed and re-echoed around the room.

The Count stared at her incredulously.

'I do not believe it!' he managed to say at last.

'It is true. She took enough laudanum to kill two strong men, and when her maid found her this morning, she must have been dead for eight or ten hours.'

'Good God!'

The Count ejaculated the words. Then forgetting all ceremony he walked across the room to stand at the window looking out onto the barren garden under a bleak November sky.

'I will do everything in my power to keep your name out of this,' the Queen Dowager said after a moment, 'and to prevent there being a scandal.'

'Why should I get involved?' the Count asked truculently.

'Because Luise had quarrelled with Willem over *you*.'

'Over me?'

'She had written a letter to you, a most indiscreet epistle, I understand, which any husband would resent.'

'How did Willem come to see it?'

'Luise was writing it in her private Sitting-Room. He entered unexpectedly and because she looked so guilty and tried to cover up the letter he took it from her by force.'

'It is the kind of thing Willem would do!' the Count said harshly.

The Queen Dowager sighed.

'You know as well as I do how insanely jealous he is, and of course where you are concerned he has had every justification.'

'It was all over two months—no, nearly

three months ago.'

'Perhaps it was from your point of view,' the Queen Dowager said, 'but Luise was still in love with you and behaved, I must admit, in an extremely hysterical manner.'

The Queen Dowager paused for a moment, then added:

'So she died.'

The Count stared blindly out at the formal gardens.

He was wishing as he had wished so many times before that he had never become involved with the Baroness van Heydberg, who had been the only attractive woman in attendance upon the Queen Dowager.

The other ladies-in-waiting were fat, middle-aged and dumpy, and even to look at them made the Count think of suet puddings and dumplings, which he had always disliked as a child.

In contrast Luise van Heydberg had been like a breath of spring on a winter's day.

She had been beautiful, slim and very young for the post she occupied by right

because her husband was of such importance at Court.

The Baron's second wife, Luise, was
young enough to be his daughter and, as
the Count quickly discovered, was not in the
least in love with the man she had married.

Since she came from a family of no social
importance, it had been for her a brilliant
marriage accepted ecstatically by her parents
who could hardly believe their good fortune.

It had not mattered to them that the Baron
was over fifty years of age or that his obses-
sion for Luise from the moment he had seen
her was likely at first to frighten, then revolt
a very young girl.

All that mattered was that as Baroness
van Heydberg she would become a hereditary lady-in-waiting to the Queen Dowager
and have a position at Court which they had
never imagined possible.

To the Count it had been just another of
his light and amusing flirtations which made
the path of duty easier than it might have
been otherwise.

He had no intention of embarking on anything serious with the wife of another man, nor did he intend, if he could help it, to add to the gossip-writers' store of incidents which they repeated and re-repeated to his disadvantage.

He had found Luise's instantaneous response to his first overtures intriguing and definitely flattering.

She had made it clear that he embodied everything she had dreamt about in her adolescent dreams and was the hero to whom she had been romantically inclined since she was a child.

'I worship you!' she had said once. 'You are like Apollo. You bring a light to the darkness of my life.'

Satiated as he was with beautiful women and with *affaires de coeur* which had occupied a great deal of his time since he was adolescent, the Count had been touched and at times moved by Luise's passion for him.

Then about three months ago he had realised it was getting out of hand.

She found it impossible, loving him as she did, to disguise her feelings even when they were surrounded by the stern, disapproving eyes of those to whom protocol was a religion.

She began to plead with him to see her more than it was possible for him to do.

She wanted to take dangerous risks so that they could be together and for him to make love to her even when her husband was in the same building, or only a room away.

The Count began to be afraid.

He felt like a man who had made a small hole in the dyke and now the whole sea was rushing in and threatening to overwhelm him and everyone else.

With an expertise which came from long practice he began to disentangle himself both metaphorically as well as physically from the clinging arms of Luise, from her lips, hungry for his kisses, from her insistent demands upon him.

She sensed, as a woman always can, what was happening.

She therefore bombarded him with letters and messages and when they were alone begged him to love her with an abandonment which made him uneasy.

Too late he realised that her nature was hysterical to the point where she could easily become unbalanced.

Too late he realised he had started an avalanche that was now out of control.

'Listen, Luise, you are a married woman,' he said over and over again. 'You have a duty to your husband. If you behave like this he will take you away to the country and we shall never see each other again.'

He thought as he spoke that it would be the best thing that could happen, but his words brought a flood of tears and protestations.

On one occasion Luise even knelt at his feet, pleading with him, begging him with the tears falling down her cheeks not to leave her.

In his dealings with women the Count had always been very much the dominant figure.

In fact his name was apt in that he was the victor, the conqueror, and the women to whom he made love invariably surrendered themselves completely to everything he demanded of them.

At the same time the majority were sensible and sophisticated enough to safe-guard their reputations.

The Count often thought cynically that it was the women who listened, even when they were at their most abandoned, for a footstep on the stairs, a creak of the door the faintest sound that might mean discovery.

He had made a mistake, he realised, in choosing someone as young as Luise, apart from the fact that her whole temperament was obviously unsuited to intrigue of any sort.

He might have been excused for not realising how she would behave in as much as she had been married for four years, given her husband the heir he craved and could therefore no longer be thought of as being a young and innocent bride.

What he had forgotten was that Luise had never, until she met him, been in love.

She was swept off her feet and like many women before her thought the world well lost as she was awakened for the first time to the ecstasy of passion.

The Count was a very experienced lover, he was also, when he made love, considerate and tender as he never was at any other time.

Men thought him ruthless and it was only in moments of intimacy that a woman could see the softer side of his nature of which at other times he was rather ashamed.

Never before in all his years of enjoying the favours of the fair sex whenever they were offered to him had he known anyone so wildly, almost insanely in love as Luise.

Aloud now, without turning round, he asked:

'What, Ma'am, does Willem intend to do about it?'

'I have already spoken to him,' the Queen Dowager said. 'He is, as might be expected, extremely bitter and would wish, if it was possible, to kill you!'

'I think that would be unlikely,' the Count remarked involuntarily.

'That is not the point,' the Queen Dowager retorted sharply. 'You know as well as I do, Viktor, if one word is known about this it will cause a scandal that will reverberate throughout Europe and harm the Queen. That is something I cannot allow.'

'No, of course not.'

'I decided when I became Regent,' the Queen Dowager went on, 'that because Wilhelmina was so young, the Court must set an example of purity and propriety.'

The Count wanted to say: 'Very commendable!' but he thought it might sound sarcastic.

The Dutch Court had, he thought, never been anything but an example of dull, uninspired Monarchy which most other Courts had no wish to emulate.

But he knew by the serious manner in which the Queen Dowager was speaking that she felt very strongly about the direction in which her duty lay.

'It is,' she was saying, 'as you can imagine, impossible for you and Willem to meet. That is why I have decided on a solution which I think will solve for the moment at any rate, his problem and yours.'

The Count turned from the window.

'What are you asking me to do?' he enquired.

'I am telling you,' the Queen Dowager replied, 'that you must leave here immediately and take a ship which I have already learnt is sailing from Zetland tonight for the East Indies.'

'The East Indies?'

The Count was so surprised that his voice as he said the words was unexpectedly loud.

'I shall inform the Privy Council that I have received disquieting news from the Island of Bali,' the Queen Dowager went on, 'and have sent you as my Personal Advisor to report what is happening in that part of the world.'

'Bali!' the Count repeated as if he had never heard of the island.

'Provided you leave to-day,' the Queen Dowager continued. 'Willem will not announce the death of his wife until to-morrow, when you will have left the country.'

'How can it be possible for him to postpone the announcement?' the Count enquired automatically.

'Fortunately the Doctor who attended Luise is one of my private Physicians,' the Queen Dowager replied, 'and he, Willem, you and I are at the moment the only persons who know Luise is dead—apart, of course, from her lady's-maid, who had been with her since she was a child and can be trusted.'

The Count said nothing and after a moment the Queen Dowager went on:

'You should be very grateful to Willem that when he found Luise was dead he came at once to ask me what he should do. As an old servant of the Crown he was aware that knowledge of his wife's action would be detrimental to the Monarchy.'

'You wish me to leave to-day?'

'If you are to catch the ship in which I intend you to travel,' the Queen Dowager said, 'you will have only a few hours in which to pack your things.'

She paused as if she expected the Count to speak. When he did not do so, she continued:

'Before you leave you will receive your credentials and the secret papers which you will carry on my behalf, and of course the names of those officials whom you will interview on arrival in Bali.'

The Count still did not say anything and the Queen Dowager thought for the first time since she had known her cousin that he seemed for the moment unsure of himself.

Looking at his handsome face, her eyes softened and there was definitely a more kindly note in her voice as she said:

'I'm sorry this has occurred, Viktor, but you have no-one to blame but yourself.'

'No-one!' the Count agreed.

★ ★ ★ ★

It was a sentence he was to repeat to himself over and over again on the voyage.

The ship in which he travelled was a comfortable one and in deference to his rank and prestige he was treated in almost a Royal manner from the moment he stepped aboard.

It was only when, during the long days and even longer nights at sea, he had time for introspection that he acknowledged his sins had caught up with him and the punishment was well deserved.

The Count was, as it happened, a highly intelligent man and while he was prepared to take the blame for Luise's death he also was aware that the same thing might have happened to any man who aroused her emotions.

Most women were unpredictable, but there were those who, taken out of the rut in which they had lived all their lives, could easily become completely out of control or to put it in one word—unhinged.

This, however, did not console the Count for having to leave his estates, his houses which he had arranged to his own satisfaction and the admiration of everyone else, and his many personal activities.

What he resented more than anything else was the boredom of the sea-voyage.

He had been more concerned about what books to bring with him than his other personal effects which he had left to his Valet.

Even so it was hard to know how to pass the time and he found the limited intelligence of the other passengers and the Captain unendurably long before they reached the Red Sea.

He had plenty of time, however, to learn something about Bali, of which he knew very little, and he discovered with some surprise that only the North part of the island had been acquired by the Dutch.

He had imagined that, as in Java, the Dutch reigned supreme but instead, most of Bali was still under the jurisdiction of the Radjas.

To the Count it was natural that the Dutch should make every effort to consolidate their Empire in the East, but from what he read he realised that the days of open aggression were frowned on and to justify a conquest the conquerors had to embrace a cause.

Motives however to satisfy both conscience and natural aggrandisement were not hard to find.

The invasion of North Bali, he understood reading between the lines, had required only a flimsy pretext obviously magnified for the occasion. When the invasion was successful it was followed by the conquest of the neighbouring island of Lombak.

The Count might be ruthless in many ways but he was human enough to dislike an unequal contest whether it was between man and man or nation and nation.

He could understand all too readily for his peace of mind that the Radjas and their retainers were brave men, but they had been no match for repeating rifles and modern cannon.

He also had a suspicion that the Dutchmen as conquerors, had been unnecessarily cruel and insensitive, and he decided that if he saw anything of which he disapproved he would not hesitate to make certain that measures were taken when he returned to Holland.

In the meantime, however, that seemed a long way off.

He had been so bored on the outward journey that he could not for the moment contemplate embarking on what he was certain would be an identically boring return.

Whatever Bali was like, he told himself, he would have to put up with it for a time, which was what the Queen Dowager wanted him to do.

He knew that, his mission in Bali accomplished, there were a great many other places that he would find of interest and not only in the immediate vicinity. It would be amusing to visit India and compare the role the British played as conquerors with that of his own countrymen.

There was also Siam which would be worth a visit, and perhaps, nearer home, Persia and Constantinople.

Those places sounded considerably more alluring than Bali and the Count cheered up at the thought of them.

He told himself, however, first things first, and as he looked around him critically he decided that the sooner he had his first report ready for the Queen Dowager, the better.

He had been met at the Port by the Governor with what seemed to be an extremely ancient conveyance drawn by horses which the Count would have thought beneath his dignity to own had he seen them in Holland.

The Governor was a large, over-weight man in his late thirties with a complexion which made the Count suspect that he imbibed too frequently and too copiously.

He spoke in the sharp, staccato manner of a man who was used to giving orders to inferiors, and the Count suspected that it was with somewhat of an effort that he made himself polite and conciliatory to his guest.

'We have been greatly looking forward to your visit, *Mijnheer*!' he said.

The Count was quite certain that was untrue, but he acknowledged the politeness with a faint smile and as they drove from the Port looked about him, in what he hoped the Governor would think was an interested manner.

He had expected because he had read about it that the women would be graceful and he saw now that he had not been mistaken.

The custom of carrying everything that needed to be conveyed on their heads had given them the carriage of a goddess and the slimness of a long-stemmed flower.

The Count was also intrigued by the fact that they were naked to the waist and the only coverings on their golden skins were bead necklaces which swung and shimmered as they moved.

Both men and women wore flowers in their hair and as if the Governor felt he should excite the Count's interest, he went into a rather lewd exaltation of the attractions of the females.

'You must see the dancing while you are here,' he said. 'That is something worth watching and I am certain, *Mijnheer*, that you will enjoy the cock-fighting.'

The Count did not reply.

That was the one sport which he found particularly unpleasant, but he knew from what he had read in his books that it had an almost obsessional interest for the Balinese and doubtless for their conquerors.

'We will do our best to entertain you,' the Governor went on, 'although I am afraid you will find life here dull and comparatively uneventful. There is no fighting here in the North. We see to that!'

He grinned and continued:

'I believe the Radjas in the South are always sparring with each other so sooner or later they will give us an excuse to step in and bring peace to the people.'

'Is that really what you expect to do?' the

Count asked with a twist of his lips.

The Governor smiled.

'For the peasant, one Ruler is very like another.'

'I doubt if that is true,' the Count commented, but he did not wish to make an issue of it.

They reached the Governor's Palace which was built in the style that could have been found in any part of the East. The large high rooms had *punkahs* swinging on every ceiling but even so the heavy moist air seemed over-powering.

It had been a long drive from the harbour but, although the Governor suggested the Count might wish to retire to his own rooms, he refused.

Instead he sat down in the large and comfortable Sitting-Room and while the Governor ordered drinks said with a note of authority in his voice:

'I am anxious while I am here to see the whole workings of your administration. The Queen Dowager has asked me to make a special report on Northern Bali.'

'I gathered that was why you had come here,' the Governor answered. 'I only hope that the report you make will make it easy for us to obtain more guns and cannon by which we can conquer the rest of the island.'

'That is not what I intend,' the Count replied, 'but I will certainly put your request forward, if that is what you wish, in my report.'

'It must certainly be the obvious conclusion to our occupation,' the Governor replied.

He was about to say more when a servant came to his side.

'What is it?' he asked testily.

'The *Juffrouw* Barclay whom you asked to visit you yesterday is now here, Your Excellency.'

'I said yesterday!' the Governor replied sharply.

'I think the *Juffrouw* will make her apologies, Your Excellency, but she could not come.'

The Governor rose to his feet.

'If you will forgive me,' he said to the Count, 'there is someone who wishes to see me.'

'Barclay does not sound a Dutch name.'

'The young lady is in fact English.'

'English? Here in Bali?'

As if he was reluctant to give information the Governor said:

'She came out here with her uncle who was Dutch and a Missionary.'

'A Missionary!'

There was no doubt that the Count was surprised.

He had read in the books he had studied on the way over that in 1877 a law had been passed forbidding any Missionary to settle in Bali.

'As you cannot be aware,' the Governor explained seeing the expression on the Count's face, 'temporary terms were accorded last year to both Catholic and Protestant Missionaries who wished to make a further attempt to carry on their work.'

'I did not know that,' the Count replied.

'It was, I believe, entirely on the instigation of the Churches at home who felt that we were lacking in our duty if we denied these heathens the benefits and comfort of Christianity.'

'I understood that the Balinese have a definite religion of their own.'

'That is true.'

'I also learnt that the plight of the first Christian convert has become legendary,' the Count said.

It was a story which the Count had found in every book he had perused about the island. The man's name had been Nicodemus and he had been both a pupil and a servant of the first Missionary who had set foot in Bali.

When the community to which he belonged learned that he had become a Christian they expelled him from his village, banned him from all contact with his people and proclaimed him morally "dead".

The unfortunate man tried to recruit other

followers but the villagers, terrorised by the threats to their Priests; ignored him.

Repulsed on all sides, poor Nicodemus had led an intolerable existence until driven to despair he had finally killed his master and given himself up to be executed.

It was not surprising, the Count thought, that a law forbidding Missionaries had come into force.

He found it hard to believe that only fourteen years later things would be so changed that Christian Missionaries would again be accepted.

He looked at the Governor and had a feeling that he was uncomfortable and was concealing something.

Making up his mind on the impulse of the moment, the Count said:

'I would like to meet this woman who has come here to see you. It would give me a chance to find out how her Mission is working.'

'It is not her mission,' the Governor said in a surly manner. 'It was her uncle's.'

'But she works with him?'

'He is dead!'

'Dead?' the Count questioned.

'He died two months ago.'

'Naturally, or was he killed?'

'Naturally.'

'Then I presume his niece is carrying on his good work. Let me talk to her.'

The Count thought the Governor was going to defy him and refuse to allow him to see the woman who was waiting outside.

It was only an impression, and yet the Count was certain he was not mistaken.

For some reason which he could not understand the Governor was very reluctant for him to come in contact with this Miss Barclay, which was the way, being English, he knew she would be addressed.

For a moment the eyes of the two men met and it was if there was a silent combat between them. Then the Governor capitulated.

'Show the *Juffrouw* in,' he said to the servant and sat down on the seat he had just vacated.

The Count was intrigued.

Had he so soon after setting foot in Bali discovered something perhaps reprehensible that the Governor had no wish for him to know about or investigate?

For the first time his boredom lightened a little and he felt a spark of interest that had not been there before.

He was amused that he had been able to assert his will over an older man who had realised at first meeting, enjoyed and took advantage of every privilege he was accorded as Governor.

Neither of the men spoke until the servant said from the doorway:

'The *Juffrouw* Roxana Barclay, Your Excellency.'

He mispronounced both English words, but the Count understood what he was trying to say. Then into the room came a slim young woman who moved with a grace that was almost that of a Balinese woman.

She seemed to float over the wooden floor towards where the Governor and the

Count were sitting.

She wore a plain white gown with a tight bodice which revealed the soft curves of her breasts and showed off the slimness of her waist.

It swept back into a small bustle, the folds of which made her look like a Grecian goddess, an image that was magnified by the way in which she held her head and by the beauty of her hair.

What astonished the Count was that she wore no hat which was extremely unconventional; but she carried a sunshade which must certainly have kept the sun's burning rays from the exquisite perfection of her white skin.

Her hair was not the ordinary gold likened by poets to a cornfield or to the rays of the sun, but was the colour of the first autumn leaves with a touch of russet in them.

It was piled into a bun at the back of her head but seemed somehow eager to escape from the confines its owner had intended, to fall in tiny tendrils round her neck and her oval forehead.

Her large eyes were green with touches of gold in them that seemed to have come from the sunshine.

She had a haunting and very unusual face, not classically beautiful, but with something far more individual, far more arresting, as if it was a face that came from a man's dreams and was not wholly human.

When Roxana Barclay came within a few feet of the Governor she curtsied.

It was a very graceful and very lovely gesture.

'Good day, Your Excellency,' she said, 'and may I offer my apologies for not calling here yesterday as you requested me to do.'

'I am used to my orders being obeyed,' the Governor said.

He spoke in a voice which the Count knew was put on for his benefit, but his eyes, when he looked at the woman facing him, said something very different.

'I did not receive your message,' Roxana

Barclay explained. 'I was away from home.'

'In the forest, I suppose?' the Governor said harshly. 'I have warned you before that it is dangerous to go wandering about on your own.'

'No-one will hurt me,' was the reply, 'and I only went to look for wood.'

'For wood?'

The Count could not help interposing the exclamation.

He could not imagine why this elegant young girl should require wood unless it was needed for cooking, in which case why could not a servant have fetched it for her?

As if she noticed his presence for the first time, Roxana Barclay looked at the man who had spoken.

With obvious reluctance the Governor said to the Count:

'May I present Miss Roxana Barclay? As I have already told you she is here on sufferance. Her uncle had a permit to remain for two years, which of course, now is terminated.'

Roxana curtsied as she was introduced and for some reason he could not explain to himself the Count rose to his feet and held out his hand.

'I am glad to make your acquaintance, Miss Barclay,' he said in English.

He saw the delight in her eyes which seemed to make them larger than they were before.

'You speak English?'

'I hope well enough for you to understand me.'

'You are being modest, *Mijnheer*, you speak perfect English. I am surprised!'

'Why?'

'I am sorry if that sounds rude. But the servant told me that I had called at an inconvenient time because a very important Dutch Official was with the Governor, and all the other officials I have met can speak only their own language.'

'What you have heard or not heard in the past cannot be of interest,' the Governor said harshly.

'I am...sorry,' Roxana murmured.

'On the contrary,' the Count contradicted. 'I am interested and I would like to know, Miss Barclay, about your work here.'

She looked puzzled.

'My...work?'

Then she smiled in understanding.

'Oh, you mean my uncle's work. It is not mine.'

'You are not a Missionary?'

'No, and I have no interest in trying to convert an already happy people into accepting a creed which is quite alien to their natures.'

'That is not the sort of thing you should say,' the Governor said sharply. 'You know as well as I do, Roxana, that it is the policy of the Dutch authorities to further Christianity, if it is at all possible.'

Again the Count knew the Governor was talking to impress. At the same time, he had not missed the familiar way in which he addressed the English girl.

Roxana ignored him. Instead she said

to the Count:

'I must explain that now my uncle is dead I am interested only in my own work.'

'And what is that?'

'I am a sculptor in wood.'

'You mean you are a carver?'

'That sounds a rather crude name for something that is an art, especially on this island.'

'I read that carving is one of the national occupations. They make the decorations for the Temples and the masks which are used for their festivals.'

The Count was rather pleased that he could show himself so knowledgeable and thought that the Governor was surprised, especially as she said:

'I see you know a great deal about the native customs, *Mijnheer*.'

'I always make it my business to know as much as possible about any place I visit,' the Count replied reprovingly. 'Will you not sit down, Miss Barclay? There are quite a number of things I would like to talk to you about and which I suspect the Balinese would not wish to tell me, and the Dutch would not want me to know!'

Roxana sat down on the chair he indicated. Then with a glance at the Governor she said:

'If I say too much, it will get me into trouble.'

'Why?'

'Because I am only here on sufferance. I believe a number of the Dutch residents have already said that now my uncle is dead I should leave the island.'

'You are living alone?'

There was an incredulous note in the Count's voice.

'Not exactly,' she replied. 'I have with me someone who I consider to be quite sufficient as a Chaperon, an elderly woman who was with my aunt for many years.'

'A servant!' the Governor said sharply.

'My aunt looked upon Geertruida as a companion, which is what she now is to me.'

The Governor sighed as if in exasperation.

'I have suggested, *Mijnheer*,' he said addressing the Count, 'that Miss Barclay, if she wishes to stay in Bali, should live with some respectable Dutch family. I could easily find her a place in one of their villas, but she will not agree.'

'I prefer to be on my own,' Roxana said. 'I work very hard and sometimes late at night. That would certainly prove an inconvenience to most people.'

'You should accept the situation I have offered to you.'

The Count was aware that Roxana stiffened. Then she said in a cold voice that she had not used before:

'What you have suggested, Your Excellency, is quite unacceptable! I would not consider it under any circumstances!'

CHAPTER TWO

Roxana was nervous.

She hoped that she showed no sign of it, at the same time, she was well aware that this newcomer might make trouble.

There had been a lot of trouble already caused by the women of the Dutch community who had said categorically that since her uncle was dead she should not be allowed to stay in Bali.

Roxana knew they were not concerned so much with her position as a young woman as that they were jealous.

It would be impossible for the fat, unattractive *Mevrouws* whose complexions had deteriorated in the sun and whose heavy eating had put many surplus pounds on their figures not to resent the way she looked.

They watched her suspiciously and they also made it clear, as they had from the time of her arrival in Bali, that they did not consider a Missionary or his relatives of any social consequence.

Roxana often thought with amusement how easily she could change their attitude by telling them who were her relatives in England and giving them the names of her father and mother.

But it would be far more dangerous for them to be interested in her and she preferred their ostracism to their patronage.

Sometimes she thought frantically that she was fighting a lone battle against an enemy that encroached on her from every side.

Then because she had a sense of humour she laughed at her own fears and told herself that in reality there was nothing to frighten her.

That was until the Governor had become a more insidious and frightening enemy than the Dutch people he ruled.

When her uncle by marriage decided to

visit Bali as a Missionary and agreed to take her with him it had seemed an adventure so intriguing, so exciting that while Roxana had said a prayer of gratitude every day until they actually sailed, she also held her breath!

She had been so afraid that something would prevent them from setting off at the last moment for the East which was to her like an El Dorado which she had imagined would always be out of her reach.

But as soon as she arrived in Holland after her father's death to stay with her Aunt Agnes, she had realised that her uncle, Pieter Helderik, was restless and at loggerheads with the small community in which they lived.

He was a brilliantly intelligent but over-sensitive man, who lived on his nerves. It made him find the daily round of parochial work dull and uninspiring.

He preached with a fire which would have galvanised anyone but the solid Dutch Burghers into which a flame of enthusiasm which would have equalled his own.

Instead they sat solidly in their pews with an expression on their faces that Roxana knew was one of disapproval.

They thought Pieter Helderik too theatrical, too dramatic, and they did not wish to feel anything about the God they worshipped except that He was there to supply their needs and be a comforting background in their uneventful lives.

'How can I move them?' Pieter Helderik said once in despair to his niece.

'I think only dynamite could do that, Uncle Pieter,' Roxana replied.

He had laughed a little ruefully.

'I try—Heaven knows I try—to enthuse the spirit of God into them, but it is rather like thumping a goose-feather mattress and I am well aware I make no impression.'

He besieged the authorities until he made the Dutch change their minds about excluding Missionaries from Bali.

He had been supported by the Catholics, and he had also aroused public opinion about the iniquities of leaving a conquered country without the solace and privilege of hearing the Christian message.

Reluctantly and with a scepticism which they did not attempt to disguise the authorities finally conceded that temporary permits should be accorded to a few specially chosen Missionaries.

These would be reviewed year by year, and very stringent conditions were laid on those to whom they were granted.

Sometimes Roxana was certain that she would not be allowed to accompany her uncle and aunt on their voyage.

But she fancied that the Dutch authorities, bored with Pieter Helderik's unceasing petitions, were actually glad to rid themselves of someone they considered an intolerable nuisance.

Whatever the reason the Helderiks and Roxana had finally set sail from Holland on a small and extremely uncomfortable steamer, but so glad to be on their way that for them it might have been the *Santa Maria* setting out with Christopher Columbus to discover a new Continent.

It was only her Aunt Agnes, Roxana thought later, who seemed unexcited at the prospects of travelling to a new country and leaving everything that was familiar behind.

She was a quiet, sweet-tempered woman who adored her husband and would in fact have followed him down into Hell if he had demanded it of her.

Roxana believed he was taking them to Paradise.

She knew from her researches about Bali that it was called "The Island of Paradise", "The Enchanted Isle", and "The Island of the Gods".

The more she read and the more she learned about Bali, the more excited she grew at the thought of actually seeing all the beauty which had stirred her imagination, but which she had always doubted if she would ever see with her own eyes.

It was only when they were passing through the Red Sea and her Aunt Agnes seemed to suffer from the heat that Roxana learned her secret.

After being married for fifteen years to Pieter Helderik she was unexpectedly and almost incredibly having a child!

'We prayed so fervently that we might be blessed,' Agnes Helderik said to her niece, 'but we had both given up hope.'

'Why did you not tell us before we left, Aunt Agnes?'

Her aunt had smiled.

'If I had done so, Pieter would have postponed our departure and they might have cancelled his permit.'

'Why should they do that?'

'The Dutch made it very clear that they would not allow Missionaries with young children to go to Bali. They did not consider it safe.'

'Aunt Agnes!' Roxana exclaimed in consternation. 'What will they say now?'

Her aunt smiled.

'Perhaps we can keep them from finding out.'

This was something Roxana had never

envisaged and she foresaw from the very moment her aunt told her the truth that there were a great many difficulties ahead.

First and most important was to keep Pieter Helderik himself from realising what was happening until they had actually landed on the island.

This was not difficult! He was in an ecstatic state of excitement about his new life and he would, Roxana thought with a smile, not have noticed if she and his wife had turned black in the night.

All he could think about—and it filled every waking hour of his day—was the work he had dedicated himself to do amongst the people of Bali.

He had already, Roxana discovered, a wide knowledge of Balinese and their customs.

He would sit on deck, whatever the weather, poring over one of the books he had brought with him, making notes, and then instructing his wife and his niece on dozens, if not hundreds, of things they must do or not do to avoid causing offence to the people among whom they were now to live.

'My head is whirling with so many different "taboos" and restrictions!' Roxana said to her aunt.

'One of our friends in Holland told us it was a "land of taboos",' Mrs Helderik replied, 'but I expect they exaggerated as people always do, and we shall find once we reach there it is very like any other place and no more difficult.'

She spoke a little wearily as if she was finding it hard to echo her husband's enthusiasm and not to let him realise that she often felt ill and was at all times very lethargic.

Roxana helped her and it was only after they had reached Bali and had settled down to the village in which they were to live that Pieter Helderik learnt the truth.

He was then torn in two by elation that after so many prayers he was to have a child and his terror that because of it he might be sent back to Holland.

It was Geertruida, Mrs Helderik's maid,

who had been with her all her married life and treated her mistress as if she was a child who needed her care, who solved everything.

'You can leave everything to me, *Juf-frouw*,' she said to Roxana. 'I have delivered many babies in the village where I was born. My mother was the midwife and when she could not attend an expectant mother I went in her place.'

'But after it is born?' Roxana questioned.

Geertruida smiled.

'There are children everywhere,' she said. 'Who would notice one more?'

That was certainly true.

Roxana had never seen so many children or such attractive ones, but she could not help feeling that among the Balinese children with their honey-gold skins, a fair-haired Dutch child, if he resembled his father, would stand out like a sore thumb.

But when Karel was born she found him so entrancing, so attractive, that she knew she would fight for him if it took every ounce of her strength and will!

That she discovered was exactly what she had to do.

Geertruida delivered Karel secretly and apparently efficiently, although she confessed it was a difficult birth and depleted Agnes Helderik of her strength.

It was, however, Roxana thought, worth all the suffering in the world for that exquisite moment when her aunt gave her son into her husband's arms.

There was something so reverent and so rapturous in his face that it was as if he knew himself blessed above all mortals and the wonder of his gift from God was beyond words.

As Roxana had gone from the room leaving the husband and wife and their new-born child together, she felt for a moment as if she had been present at the Nativity and half-expected to see the Star of Bethlehem shining in the sky above them.

But their happiness was short-lived.

Mrs Helderik developed a fever for which Geertruida had no cure and she grew weaker day by day.

Even so Roxana was not really alarmed until one morning she learnt that her aunt had died quietly in the night while they had all been asleep.

There was a smile on her lips and she could not have suffered.

She had in fact slipped away and left Geertruida and Roxana with the month-old Karel on their hands and a husband who was completely broken-hearted.

What made things so difficult was that while the funeral took place and quite a number of people came to express their condolences, Karel had to be hidden away.

It was not for some months that Roxana realised that in dying her aunt had left a void in the life of her husband which could never be filled.

Because she was so quiet, so gentle and unassuming it had been easy for Roxana, like many other people they knew, to consider Agnes Helderik of little account and certainly of no importance.

When against her father's wishes she married the man she loved, and adored him in a manner which made her completely subservient to his every wish, Agnes had cut herself off completely from the life she had lived as a girl in England.

She was the daughter of a land-owner with a considerable Estate who was of consequence in his own County and also had a great number of friends in London, and her father had expected that both his daughters would make advantageous marriages.

Roxana's mother had certainly done so in marrying Lord Barclay who although much older than his wife, was an important figure in the Social World.

That Agnes should have preferred a penniless Dutch Missionary was beyond her father's comprehension and that of her relatives.

'God knows where she met the man!' her father had ejaculated over and over again.

But they had met and fallen in love in a way, Roxana was to learn later, which made it impossible for either of them to be aware there was anyone else in the world.

Agnes had run away with her Dutch Missionary and even her elder sister had thought it regrettable and decided that in future as they had nothing in common there would be no point in keeping in close touch with each other.

Only as she grew up had Roxana become intrigued with the idea of her aunt living in Holland, cut off from the world she had known as a girl, but apparently with no regrets.

The family heard from Agnes Helderik at Christmas and on their birthdays, but Roxana suspected that while her aunt wrote to her sister her mother was usually too indifferent or too lazy to reply.

When Roxana realised that she must leave her home and go somewhere, anywhere, to get away from the unfortunate atmosphere in which she found it impossible to live, she had thought of her aunt.

Only one year after Lord Barclay's death

Roxana's mother had decided to marry again.

It was understandable that she should wish to do so.

At forty she was still a very attractive woman and she had spent the last six years of her life nursing a senile old man who seldom opened his mouth except to complain.

Fortunately they were rich enough to be able to afford nurses, but even so their whole way of life had been restricted and in a way unpleasant.

The moment one entered the front door it was impossible not to be aware that its owner was dying and taking an "unconscionable time" about it.

Roxana had been extremely sorry for her mother. At the same time she found it hard not to be shocked that her mother welcomed flirtatiously any man who was prepared to pay her court.

When finally she told her daughter she was to marry again, Roxana had waited for the blow to fall and had known even before her mother said who her future husband was to be that it meant she must go away.

'Not Patrick Grenton, Mama!' she had exclaimed involuntarily.

'Why not?' Lady Barclay asked coldly. 'You know as well as I do that he has been devoted to me for a long time and I am sure that we shall be very happy together.'

With difficulty Roxana bit back the protest that came to her lips.

How could she explain to her mother that while Patrick had been calling on Lady Barclay and flattering her with his attentions he had also been pursuing her daughter?

She had disliked Patrick Grenton from the first moment she had seen him.

A hard-riding, hard-drinking country Squire, he had followed her out hunting, keeping away other men who would wish to ride by her side.

In the summer he always managed to turn up unexpectedly in the woods or anywhere else when she happened to be walking or riding alone.

It was some time before Roxana became aware that Patrick Grenton was playing a double game.

Then the manner in which her mother welcomed him to the house when he called, the trouble she took over her appearance, the coy manner in which she spoke to him revealed the truth.

It was not difficult for Roxana to realise that while she attracted Patrick Grenton as a woman, the wealthy Lady Barclay was more alluring as a wife.

The mere idea that he could be so two-faced made Roxana feel sick.

Patrick was five years younger than her mother, but that did not count beside the fact that he was well known to be always hard up.

Once they were married her mother would be able to provide him with the new hunters he needed and all the comforts which owing to the raffish way he lived he was unable to afford.

'I must get away!' Roxana told herself. 'I cannot live in the house with Mama and Patrick Grenton!'

The idea of his being her Stepfather was bad enough, but she had the uncomfortable feeling that even when he was married to her mother he would still seek her out, still pursue her as he had done before.

It was, however, difficult to know where she could go.

She had a great number of friends but she could hardly stay with any of them indefinitely. And she did not wish to make her mother feel uncomfortable by deliberately asking her cousins or her father's relatives if she could make her home with them.

It seemed like an inspiration when the idea came to her that she should contact her aunt in Holland.

After all, everyone would understand that she should wish to go away when her mother first married, and what more plausible explanation could she give than that she had been invited to stay with her mother's sister?

Without mentioning her idea to a soul, Roxana had sat down and written to Agnes Helderik, asking her if she could come to Holland and saying how she longed to make her acquaintance.

The letter which had come in response had been enthusiastically welcoming, and although her mother had been astonished, Roxana had left England as soon as the quiet wedding between Lady Barclay and Patrick Grenton had taken place.

Patrick Grenton had in fact objected more strongly than his wife.

'Why do you want to go away?' he had asked angrily when he learned of Roxana's plans. 'I want you here! I want to see you and talk to you.'

'I have no wish to play gooseberry to you and Mama,' Roxana answered.

He had looked at her and she disliked the expression in his eyes.

'You know it is not like that,' he said.

'I know what it is like and I do not wish to discuss it,' Roxana said coldly.

'Suppose I refuse to let you go?'

'You cannot prevent me.'

'Are you sure about that? After all, as your Stepfather I am also your Guardian.'

'I have every intention of leaving this house as soon as you and Mama are married, and I advise you not to make a fuss!'

Roxana spoke in a manner which brought the anger into his eyes and his lips tightened.

'If that is your attitude about the future,' he said, 'then sooner or later I will make you regret it!'

She did not bother to answer him. She only looked at him with contempt, but when she left the room she had heard him swearing in a manner which made her shiver.

However she found her aunt, Roxana was determined to like her, and stay with her for as long as possible. Holland was at least a refuge from Patrick Grenton.

Actually she had loved Mrs Helderik from the first moment she met her and her aunt had loved her.

She was, Roxana thought, exactly what

she would have wished her mother to be like, but Lady Barclay had grown hard during the frustrating years of her late husband's incurable illness.

Lady Barclay had, at first, despite the disparity in their ages, been very happy.

Lord Barclay had been an extremely intelligent man who had given distinguished service to the Crown and was greatly respected in political circles.

But when he became ill he was like an oak that had been struck by lightning.

If only he could have died after the first ten years of marriage, it would have been easy for everyone to mourn him in genuine sorrow.

Instead he had lingered on and through no real fault of his own had gradually lost his friends and the love of his wife and daughter.

It had been wrong, Roxana knew, to be glad when someone died, and yet when, wearing the deepest black, she followed her father's coffin to the graveside, she had known that the trappings were only a farce.

It was a relief that after so long he was freed of his tortured body, but Roxana had cried at her aunt's death as she had never been able to do for her father.

It seemed so cruel, so unnecessary, that when she was so ecstatically happy at having given her husband the son he had longed for, after so many years, Agnes Helderik had died.

But if Roxana was unhappy it was nothing compared to the overwhelming grief suffered by Pieter Helderik.

He had not only adored his wife with his whole heart and soul, but she was also a part of him, completely necessary both to his mind and body.

He was like a rudderless ship and it was true, Roxana thought, to say that the light had gone out of his life.

He flung himself into his work in Bali with no less enthusiasm and a one-pointed concentration that was characteristic of his personality, but from the day Agnes died something was missing.

Before her death everything he had said and done had been spontaneous and seemed to come almost as if it was an inspiration from above. Now he drove himself and at times Roxana even thought he was pretending to feel what was not actually there.

She could not put her finger on exactly what was wrong, and yet she knew that her aunt from the moment she died, had taken with her something that was indispensable to Pieter Helderik.

Soon after coming to Bali Roxana had seen and understood clearly why the Dutch had been reluctant to issue even temporary permits to Missionaries.

She had known without anyone telling her that the intransigence of the inhabitants in religious matters doomed all the Missionaries' efforts to failure.

All she had read about Bali and all she saw from her own observations made her realise that the Priests, the *pedandas* would not tolerate that any member of their race should go over to a new religion.

When there were Christian converts, although they were very few, they were boycotted and usually hunted out of the community.

Balinese doctors refused to treat Christians and they were threatened that if they died they would not be allowed to be buried in Balinese cemeteries.

She tried tactfully to tell Pieter Helderik what was happening, but he would not listen and pretended that he did not believe her. But it was obvious that he was shunned when he moved about the villages.

The Balinese, usually a smiling, easy-going people, vanished into their thatched houses when he appeared or deliberately moved away when he attempted to speak to them.

It was only the children who were not afraid and were not concerned with anything except that he would give them sweetmeats and occasionally buy them toys.

'It is hopeless! Quite hopeless!' Roxana

told herself over and over again.

But she dare not say it aloud for fear of hurting her uncle more than he had been hurt already.

She knew he was aware of what was happening because the lines on his face sharpened and he grew thinner and thinner until the clothes he had brought with him from Holland hung on him as if he was a scarecrow.

He found it hard to eat even the delicious dishes that Geertruida prepared and which had been his favourites at home.

He took to wandering off, moving through the woods and fields as if he was a ghost or, as the Balinese would have said, a *leyak* of which they were all afraid.

The Balinese had such a deep fear of evil spirits that Roxana knew that for someone to be associated in their minds with Leyak was definitely dangerous.

It meant they thought he "danced in the flames, haunted graveyards, and the older people believed he would be re-incarnated in the bodies of dangerous beasts such as tigers, monkeys and sharks".

She heard that a man fated to become a *leyak* began by learning by heart the words of the ancient manuscripts.

She thought that Pieter Helderik as he wandered through the woods repeated aloud to himself the prayers which sometimes sustained him but often sounded like the anguished confessions of a penitent, would frighten any Balinese who heard him.

Roxana was quite certain that something was seriously wrong as her uncle began to weaken and return home from his wanderings completely exhausted, to refuse all food and just lie in his bed staring vacantly into space.

'He looks like a man bewitched!' Geertruida said one day.

Roxana knew that she put into words what she herself had been afraid to acknowledge even in her thoughts.

In England or Holland she would have laughed at the idea, but in Bali, knowing the power of the Priests, and the universal belief in Black Magic, she was aware that things happened which could not be explained in ordinary terms.

Two months ago Pieter Helderik had not returned from one of his walks.

They found him dead in the woods, and Roxana was certain that he had died not normally but through supernatural means.

Yet what was the point of voicing such suspicions? If she did, what could anybody do about it?

When Pieter Helderik had been buried in the Dutch Cemetery, Roxana was confronted with a problem that was so frightening she did not know how to cope with it.

The Dutch authorities had made it a rule that any orphans among the community in Bali should be taken to an Orphanage either on the island or in Java.

The idea of Karel being put in an Orphanage and brought up without love and affection, was to Roxana horrifying. She knew too that if her Aunt Agnes were alive it would break her heart to think of it.

Because she loved her aunt and her uncle she was determined their child should have the advantages that should be his as his mother's son.

There were, Roxana knew, relatives in England who would look after him and care for him once she could get him there.

The difficulty was—how?

To confess now that they had deceived the Dutch authorities by allowing him to be born without acknowledging his existence and without registering the birth would be a heinous crime.

It would certainly react, not only on herself, but also on Karel.

The Dutch would first prevent the child from leaving the island unless he went to an Orphanage in Java: they would then expel her so that she must return home alone.

Once she left Karel it might take years to persuade those in charge of him to give him up, and she was not certain whether her aunt's family would even have any right to do this, considering that Karel had Dutch nationality.

It was a problem which frightened her, but made her sure that the only safe thing as far as the child was concerned, was to keep his existence a secret.

She had been fortunate in finding a family in the forest who had taken Karel into hiding after Pieter Helderik's death when the Dutch officials were continually in and out of the house.

Soon after she had come to Bali, Roxana had discovered wood-carving.

She had been very interested in sculpture when she lived in England and despite her mother's opposition, had insisted on having some lessons in moulding in clay.

It was only when she saw the Balinese carving wood which grew in profusion in their forests that she realised that this was where her real talent lay.

Up in the hills she found that many of the traditional wood-carvers had houses hidden amongst the trees where they worked, a sculptor's knife in their hands for all the hours of day-light.

Holding a block of wood fast between their bare feet they carved assiduously, bent over their work.

She watched some of them hewing into shape large blocks of Sawo which was a dark red wood, used for carving dancers and buffaloes.

Others worked in teak which Roxana learnt was particularly suitable for portraying female figures or long-necked deer.

The more skilful carvers chiselled with a genius for precision and detail the Youthful Vishus astride winged *garudas* with human legs.

These figures which were small and often miniature in size were carved in the deliciously scented sandalwood.

Roxana looked around for a teacher and found one in Ida Anak Temu.

He was a withered little man but she realised that all the other carvers spoke of him with respect and the young men with awe.

She begged him to teach her and when

he saw the work her fingers could do he accepted her as a pupil and she found a new happiness and a new interest which was different from anything she had known before.

The Balinese invariably painted their carvings, colouring them in the brilliant reds, blues, yellows and greens which were traditional for the decoration of the Temples and the masks that were worn at Festivals.

A red dragon with golden wings and huge white fangs curling from his upper and lower jaws and a golden crown upon his head could be very spectacular, as could a winged demon as it stood on a pedestal carved with leering face.

All the carving in Bali was intended to be gilded and painted.

Jaguars' heads, dancing figures and often exaggerated carvings of insects and animals, were all done first in the various naked woods, then painted in the most violent colours their creators could find.

Blue, red, yellow, black and white were all finished with gold leaf and every Temple was a kaleidoscope of colour which was beautiful in European eyes only six months later when it had been mellowed by the moist air.

It took Roxana only a very little time to realise that the woods themselves were so beautiful there was no need to embellish them.

When she told Ida Anak Temu that she did not intend to paint what she had carved he looked at her first in astonishment. Then as if the artist in him understood her decision, he had nodded his head and made no effort to dissuade her.

It was to Ida Anak Temu that she confided her problem with regard to Karel.

She thought it was typical of the Balinese courtesy and understanding that when she had said she wished to hide the child from the Dutch authorities he had offered his help without asking any questions.

The Balinese hated their Dutch overlords.

It was not only the cruelty and repressive policy of their conquerors that they resented, it was the fact that they had been an independent people and preferred the tyranny of the Radjas to the humiliation of being under the yoke of a foreigner.

'We take the child, my wife and I. He be safe and happy in our home,' Ida Anak Temu said.

Roxana had learned enough Balinese to understand his kindness and generosity.

She thanked him, the gratitude in her eyes, and the tone of her voice making what she said more easily understood than the actual words.

That night she had led the way from the village into the woods with Geertruida carrying Karel in her arms.

It had been an eerie and a little frightening amongst the dark trees, but the moonlight had shown them the path climbing over the rough stones until finally they saw the lights of Ida Anak Temu's house ahead.

He had lowered the bamboo matting which gave them a privacy which was unusual in Balinese homes.

Inside by the light of one flickering oil-lamp they had handed Karel over and Ida Anak Temu's wife had taken the sleeping child in her arms and held him protectively in a manner which told Roxana that he would be safe and happy.

It had been easy for her to see Karel by continuing her lessons with Ida Anak Temu so that no-one was suspicious if they saw her walking up to the house.

Because after Pieter Helderik's death there was a new menace and a new problem in her life, she did not dare bring him back to the village.

This was the very real one in the person of the Governor, *Mijnheer* van Kaerstock!

She had met him on a number of occasions when Pieter Helderik had been summoned peremptorily to the Governor's house and again when after a year he had to renew his permit.

It was then that Roxana had instinctively sensed danger in the way that the Governor looked at her.

He had insisted in a manner she thought unnecessary on long conversations and complicated questionnaires.

Afterwards he had called several times at their house to enquire ostensibly after their well-being, but she had known that the only person in whom he was interested was herself.

She was however, not afraid because she had the protection of her uncle and she thought it unlikely that the Governor would dare make advances to her while she was with him.

Yet on his death, it was as if her defences were swept away and because of Karel she knew how vulnerable she was without them.

It had not taken the Governor long to come to the point.

There was, he said, a place in his office that could be admirably filled by a woman who spoke both English and Dutch.

He was in constant communication, he told, her with the English in Singapore and he needed someone to translate his letters from one language into another.

It all sounded very plausible, but Roxana had only to look at the expression in the Governor's eyes and to feel the vibrations that reached out towards her and know he had very different ideas.

She refused him politely.

'As Your Excellency is aware, I am interested in my wood-carving,' she told him, 'and I wish to continue not only with the tuition I am receiving but also with my sculptures.'

'I will see you have plenty of time for your hobbies while you are working for me.'

'It is kind of Your Excellency, but I have no need for paid employment.'

'You can afford not to?'

It was a rude question but she answered it with courtesy.

'I have a private income of my own.'

This surprised him and she was sure he had thought that he would be able to put pressure on her to do what he wanted simply because she could not afford to refuse.

'Perhaps you should return to England, now that your uncle is dead.'

He was only saying that, she knew, to frighten her. He had no wish personally for her to leave.

'I am very happy here in Bali.'

'I am not certain that I can permit you to stay.'

It was a threat she did not challenge, but it had been made and she knew it would be made again and again.

When she received the Governor's instructions the previous day to come to his house she had known that he had every excuse to send for her because she had now been in Bali for two years.

She had been hoping almost against hope that he would forget the length of her stay and that she could no longer shelter behind the temporary permit issued to Pieter Helderik.

When the summons arrived she had been spending the day ostensibly with Ida Anak Temu but actually playing with Karel.

He was now sixteen months old and growing more attractive every day.

He recognised her when she appeared and held out his small fat arms trying to say her name but finding it easier to murmur sounds he heard from the other children.

He was a fat, laughing, happy child, and holding him close against her Roxana vowed that she would never allow him to be incarcerated in one of the austere Dutch Orphanages where she was certain life was as stolid, dull and unimaginative as the people who administered them.

The Balinese children who played round them, belonging to Ida Anak's sons and daughters, looked like small golden cupids drawn by Fragonard.

There was no need to question if they were happy.

The Balinese were the happiest people in the world, and as the children played imaginative games amongst the tree-trunks and their toys were pieces of discarded wood, painted in briliant colours, it was impossible to imagine that any place could be more of a Paradise for children.

'You must stay here, Karel, but one day I will take you to England,' Roxana said.

The words were almost in the nature of a vow. Karel looking up at her gurgled happily, putting up one of his dimpled hands to touch her cheek.

★ ★ ★ ★

Now, sitting in the Governor's sitting-room, which seemed a replica of the formal parlour in Holland, Roxana looked at the Count.

She thought only with a sudden sinking inside her, that here was yet another enemy; another official who constituted a danger to Karel and to herself.

Her brain working quickly reckoned that if this new-comer became too officious, too interfering, she could, as a last resort, appeal to the Governor.

But she had a very good idea what his price would be and she was afraid even to think of it.

Because she had a natural and inescapable grace she appeared, sitting on the chair beside the Count, to be completely at her ease.

She might have been meeting him in her mother's Drawing-Room, with nothing more important behind the words they spoke to each other, than the change in the weather or the prospects of a day's hunting.

In actual fact every nerve in her body was tense and her mind was prepared to dissect and consider every question he put to her in case it was a trap.

'You like living in Bali, Miss Barclay?' the Count asked.

'I find it very interesting and very rewarding from my own point of view.'

'You mean for your wood-carving?'

'Yes. I am having lessons from one of the greatest sculptors on the island.'

'He is really good?'

She fancied there was a sneer behind the words and replied:

'I think if his work was exhibited in London or Amsterdam it would undoubtedly be acclaimed.'

'I had no idea we had such a genius amongst us!' the Governor interposed. 'One day I must visit this man and see his work for myself.'

'I think Your Excellency would find it a difficult place to reach,' Roxana said quickly. 'But I am sure he would be deeply honoured to bring some examples of his carving here to you.'

She realised she had made a mistake in commending Ida Anak Temu. She told herself that every word she spoke might be incriminating and she must be much more careful.

'And do you consider your work, Miss Barclay, to be the equal of his?' the Count enquired.

She thought he was being sarcastic and replied:

'I would not presume to be the equal of the Balinese who have carved in many families for generation after generation.'

'At the same time, you are pleased with your work?'

'I can see that there is plenty of room for improvement,' Roxana replied.

'I would like to be in the position to judge what you are doing and if, as you say, it is important that you should remain in this country.'

Roxana drew in her breath.

She felt the Count was making it clear that he agreed with the Dutch women that her presence was unnecessary.

Because she was so frightened she raised her eyes to the Governor.

'Please...Your Excellency,' she pleaded, 'renew my...permit.'

As she spoke she saw the glint in his eyes and knew he was delighted that she was forced to be a supplicant for his favour.

'My decision will rest for the moment,' he said, 'until the Count has inspected your work. I am quite sure he is an authority on carving.'

It was now the Count and not Roxana who suspected that the Governor was being sarcastic.

The Count actually had a large collection of statues in his possession which were of great artistic value.

He had bought a number of them in Rome and some in Greece and it came to his mind that he would like to show them to Roxana and compare her work to them.

There was something about her which made him think of the statue of Aphrodite that he had purchased in Athens.

It had been damaged but the perfect lines of the breasts and the hips were intact.

He had often stood in front of it and thought that it gave him a sense of satisfaction and completeness which nothing else in his collection was able to do.

Amongst his many loves there had been no-one who had made him feel as he did about the statue of Aphrodite.

And yet, he thought now, there was something about Roxana which reminded him irresistibly of that fragment of marble.

'As His Excellency the Governor suggests,' he said aloud, 'I should be interested to see your work.'

As if she realised the interview was at an end, Roxana rose to her feet.

'At what time will you call tomorrow, *Mijnheer?*' she enquired.

'Some time in the morning,' the Count replied.

Roxana curtsied.

She glanced at the Governor and saw the expression in his eyes that made her recoil as if from a snake.

Then she curtsied again and without speaking, walked from the room.

CHAPTER THREE

The Count, riding one of the small Balinese horses, reached the village where he was told Roxana lived.

On either side of the street were deep ditches and beyond them an unbroken line of high mud walls crowned with thatch and punctuated by tall, elaborately carved gateways.

Some of the streets through which he passed were dark green tunnels beneath over-arching trees.

There were children playing by every roadside as naked as the day they were born and lean dogs leaping at him in and out of gateways.

Fighting cocks in their baskets made a pattern of sound and colour close to the walls.

He had learned that a fighting cock must never be bored and so they were placed by their owners on the streets so that they could watch the passers-by.

There was red hibiscus and purple bougainvillea everywhere and the fallen frangipani blossoms made a carpet of white on the roadway through which his horse picked his way.

Outside the village he recognised Roxana's house by the description given him surlily and in a disagreeable tone by the Governor.

It was, in fact, His Excellency who had reminded him at breakfast that they were to visit Roxana Barclay and see her carvings.

'She is a talented young woman,' the Governor said genially, 'which is the reason, despite the protests from the older ladies of the Dutch community, I have not made her leave the country.'

The Count was shrewd enough to be certain there was another reason for the Governor's leniency.

He was not surprised when he saw the

guests who had been invited to meet him at last night's dinner-party.

The Governor's wife was in Holland visiting her parents and the wife of the Chief Minister took her place.

She was a large, fat, dull woman and the Count had met her counterpart a thousand times at banquets in Holland.

With the soft darkness outside the brilliant stars overhead and the fragrance of flowers coming in through the open windows, it seemed incongruous that he must spend his time making himself pleasant to the unimaginative bourgeois Dutch who had nothing to talk about except their own petty parochial affairs.

It was obvious to the Count that they had no real interest in the country they had acquired and found even the exquisite carved Temples, which they had inherited like the Balinese customs from the Hindus who originally settled on the island, uninspiring.

Then he told himself it was to be expected

that these exiles from their native land would make little attempt to interest themselves in the dreamlike quality of the people over whom they ruled.

He could quite understand that what the Dutch women resented was not that Roxana was unchaperoned but that she looked so lovely.

Beauty, wherever it was found, always aroused female jealousy, and because he was perceptive the Count was aware that where the Governor was concerned, it aroused something very different.

He made up his mind during the night that if he was to learn anything important about the Balinese he could not hope to do so in the presence of the Governor.

He therefore said firmly, as he helped himself to a piece of deliciously ripe papaya:

'I think, Your Excellency, I would prefer to visit Miss Barclay alone and also see the villages and those who live in them without their being over-awed by your august presence.'

He did not wish to sound patronising, but he saw the flash of anger in the Governor's eyes before he replied:

'I feel it is my duty to escort you and make sure of your safety.'

'I cannot believe that my life would be in any danger,' the Count replied.

He knew that the reports which had been sent back to Holland had stressed over and over again that there was no local resistance in the part of Bali occupied by the Dutch.

'The people,' one communique had said, 'have settled down under their new Rulers with complacency and without any sign of rebellion.'

Because the Governor paused before replying the Count said:

'I would like if possible to ride. I need the exercise and I also think as there are few roads that I shall be better able to see the countryside.'

He refused to be escorted by a groom and as he set off alone from Government House he knew that he left behind a feeling of resentment and anger.

But he was not perturbed.

He was so used in life to having his own way that other people's feelings, if they came into opposition with his own, did not concern him.

Now, when he saw a compound surrounded by a high mud wall topped with thatch and a tall doorway surmounted by the cross, he knew he had found Roxana's home.

Remembering how graceful and unusually lovely she was he felt a new interest stir in him.

For the first time since he had left Holland he felt alive in a way that he could not explain to himself, but which was a feeling usually connected with the treasures with which he had embellished his houses and perhaps, if he was truthful, the onset of a new love-affair.

He dismounted and led his horse through the gate-way into the central court-yard.

There were as expected, various *balés*— light bamboo structures covered with thatched roofs—and inevitably a temple dedicated to the ancestral gods.

He was aware in this instance that the shrine, which was an ancient one, would be empty, without flowers and the offerings of food with which daily every Balinese embellished his personal temple.

There were tall coconut palms and such a riot of red hibiscus and purple bougainvillea that he thought the place was a fitting shrine for Roxana herself.

Even as he thought of her she came from one of the thatched buildings, followed by a small Balinese boy who ran to take the Count's horse from him.

'Good-morning, Miss Barclay!'

She curtsied, then asked in a tone of surprise:

'You have come alone?'

'As you see,' the Count replied, 'although His Excellency was very anxious to accompany me.'

He saw the colour rise in Roxana's cheeks and knew he had been right in what he had thought.

'Will you come to what I call my studio?' she asked quickly, as if she had no desire to discuss the Governor with him.

'Of course,' the Count answered.

She turned and walked ahead and as he looked at the smallness of her waist above the elegant bustle of her cotton gown he thought that she was very well dressed for a Missionary.

He wondered how she paid for such a gown which his experienced eye knew was not home-made.

What Roxana called her Studio was a large *balé* with a wooden floor raised about three feet from the ground and covered with a thick palm-thatch.

It had the usual bamboo blinds which when lowered could make a closed wall of any of its four sides.

Now there was only one that was in place as a protection against the sun.

The Count, thinking of Roxana's work, had been certain that she would carve the small figures that were described in the books he had read and which were familiar all over the East.

They were usually of little animals or mythical characters that were half-god and half-man, or charms like a fish or a winged turtle.

When he stepped onto the raised floor he thought at first that Roxana had nothing to show him but the wood that had been brought from the forest and had obviously required a far greater strength than hers to be set in place.

Then he saw that some of the pieces of wood had already been carved and depicted figures of people and animals that seemed to have been grown out of the wood itself.

Because he was very knowledgeable about sculpture, and because of his particular liking for that of the Ancient Greeks, he realised almost instantly that he was seeing something very different from what he expected.

For a moment he was silent, then he asked:

'Is this your work or that of your teacher?'

'It is mine,' Roxana answered.

The Count walked to where a large block of *sawo* depicted the torso of a man.

He realised it was not completely finished, and yet the muscles of the man's back, the angle at which he held his head was so real, so brilliantly executed, that it was as if the figure was alive and just about to move.

The Count stared at it in astonishment, then he saw next door to it a figure of a woman carved in teak.

It was about three feet in height and the woman was kneeling on the ground, naked to the waist with her hands raised in the traditional attitude of prayer.

But instead of the traditional bent head and down-cast eyes she was looking as if at some sudden inspiration from the sky above her.

The Count was knowledgeable enough to know that Roxana had used the natural curves of the wood and the very grain to depict the grace of the model, but there was something more than that in the expression on the girl's face.

There was awe, rapture, and an ecstasy that came not only from what she saw but what she felt within her.

The Count was silent, astonished, and at the same time was moved in a manner that before he had only associated with his statue of Aphrodite.

One part of his mind tried to criticise the carving, but the thin fingers, the line of the throat, the curve of her breasts were all perfect and his eyes kept returning to the expression on the girl's face.

With an effort he turned away, still without speaking, to look at the figure of a young deer raising its head to scent danger, its body tense, its eyes wary.

'How can you have learnt all this so quickly?' he asked.

'It was in me before I came to Bali,' Roxana explained. 'I could feel it in my mind and in my fingers, but I never had the opportunity to carve until now nor a teacher to instruct me.'

'The one you have chosen must be an exceptional man.'

'He is!'

The Count turned to look at her, his eyes sweeping over her as if he was still unsure that she was in fact the creator of what stood around them.

How was it possible, he asked himself, that anyone so delicate, so fragile, could sculpt like a man and have a vision that he would not have expected to find in an old and experienced craftsman, least of all in a woman?

As if she understood his bewilderment Roxana smiled and said:

'Perhaps you would like to see the little presents I make for those who are kind to me?'

She moved as she spoke towards a table and on it the Count saw there were the small carvings he had expected her to execute but even so they were different from anything he had seen before.

Roxana picked up one and gave it to him.

It was the hand obviously of a Balinese woman almost life-size, the fingers curved slightly and delicately beautiful in its very simplicity.

There was also a child's hand, fat and dimpled and made in sandalwood.

'I love working with sandalwood,' Roxana said as the Count did not speak. 'My own hands smell of it for hours afterwards, and I always feel it has all the magic of the East in its fragrance.'

The Count put down the hand and picked up the figure of a goddess. All around the base of the small statue, serpents and apes chased each other in crazy revelry.

The goddess herself reminded him a little of Roxana and abruptly, without using his usual diplomatic politeness, he asked:

'May I buy this from you?'

Roxana shook her head.

'Nothing here is for sale.'

'Why not?'

'Because they are mine...because I have no wish to...lose them.'

The Count thought that was what he would feel about his own treasures but because he wished to possess the goddess he said:

'Is that not rather selfish?'

Roxana smiled.

'My uncle was so Christian that he was ready to give away the shirt off his back. I grew selfish out of sheer necessity and now it has become a habit.'

'I would still like to buy this goddess!'

'Then let me give it to you.'

'You know I cannot accept such a generous present.'

'Why not?' she asked. 'Are you afraid of being accused of bribery and corruption?'

It had not entered the Count's mind, but now he said:

'Perhaps that is a good idea. If I am in your debt, I can hardly be so ungallant as immediately to suggest that you should leave the island.'

His eyes met hers. Then she said in a different tone:

'Please...do not send me...away.'

'I have no power to do so,' the Count answered. 'I can only advise the Governor.'

'Then please advise him that I should... stay.'

There was a little pause before Roxana added:

'There is so much more I want to learn.'

'I cannot imagine what it could be,' the Count answered. 'Let me tell you in all sincerity that I am lost in admiration of your work.'

She looked at him as if to see that he was speaking truthfully, then she said hesitatingly:

'You...really think it is...good?'

'It is more than good,' he replied. 'You have a genius, Miss Barclay, and I am not speaking lightly, for sculpture.'

He felt he had not convinced her and went on:

'I own some very fine statuary myself and

I am not speaking in ignorance when I tell you your work is outstanding!'

He saw the expression of delight in Roxana's face and said:

'When you have completed more I should like to arrange an exhibition of your work in Amsterdam.'

'I would prefer it to be in London.'

'Again you are being selfish.'

'As it happens,' Roxana said, 'I have no desire to exhibit anywhere. I sculpt to please myself because I have an urge which cannot be denied.'

'I think that is what all artists feel,' the Count said quietly.

He walked back to the torso of the man he had first seen.

'What made you do this?' he enquired.

Roxana was silent for a moment and he thought she was debating within herself whether she would answer him truthfully. Then she said almost as if the words were dragged from her:

'When I...see a piece of wood...I can...

feel what is in it...what it can portray... even before I...touch it.'

The Count was silent knowing that was what all great sculptors felt.

Michelangelo, Canova—it was the material with which they were working which essentially dictated not only the pattern of the finished master-piece, but the way in which it should be carved.

He looked again at the girl in prayer and saw that it appeared not to have been carved but to have evolved from the natural growth of the wood.

He put out his hand to touch the smooth head and the thrown-back neck.

As he did so he felt as if he touched Roxana herself and he wondered if the softness of her skin would quiver beneath the sensuousness of his fingers.

She moved away from him to where there was a large block of wood at present untouched.

It was teak and had the smooth beauty that was characteristic of the teak which came from the forests of Bali.

She was standing looking at it and when the Count walked to her side he asked:

'What are you seeing?'

'What does it mean to you?' she replied.

'Ladies first!' he answered.

She gave him the quick smile of a child amused by a game.

'I am not certain,' she said, 'but I think that inside asking to be released is the figure of a *Lelong* dancer.'

As soon as she had spoken the Count saw that that was exactly what the wood promised: the supple, half-naked body, the elaborate jewelled and gilt headdress, the movement of thin, delicate hands following the ritual of the centuries-old dance.

'One thing I promise you,' he said quietly. 'You will not be allowed to leave Bali until that is completed!'

He heard Roxana draw in her breath as if in relief.

Then in a lighter tone she replied:

'Perhaps I must be like patient Penelope,

undoing at night what I have done during the day, so that my work shall never be finished.'

'A somewhat difficult task in wood!'

She smiled at him again and he sensed that the reverse with which she had regarded him since he had first entered the court-yard was no longer there.

She looked around at the statues and said:

'I never expected it...but I think you understand why this means so...much to me.'

'I do understand,' the Count replied, 'and perhaps one day I shall be able to show you why I can understand.'

The words came to his lips without his really considering that he should say them.

But he had a sudden vision of Roxana moving among his favourite treasures, looking up at his pictures, touching his statues, understanding as few women had ever understood why he wished to own them.

His eyes were on her face, and as if the expression in them made her a little shy she said quickly:

'I apologise. I have been very remiss in not first offering you some refreshment. The Balinese would be horrified at my bad manners.'

'I would like, if it is no trouble, something cool to drink,' the Count replied. 'I find it very hot, but I dare say I shall soon get used to the climate.'

'You intend to stay long?'

'That depends...' he replied evasively.

Roxana stepped down from where her statues rested and led the way into a *balé*.

Again the floor was raised from the ground and there were bamboo screens on three sides and it might in structure have been the home of an ordinary villager.

But as a concession to the West there were several armchairs, a table and two carved chests which stood against the bamboo walls.

There were vases of flowers which would not have been seen in any Balinese home and a book-case filled with a number of volumes most of which had been in Roxana's luggage when she left Holland.

The Count thought, as they seated themselves and a small girl was sent to tell Geertruida what they required, that strangely enough Roxana did not appear out of place.

She seemed to blend in with her surroundings almost as if she were a piece of wood which stood in her Studio.

There was a "rightness" about her, the Count thought, which would have made her fit in wherever she might be, and yet still she would be individual and unusual.

'Tell me about yourself,' he suggested.

'Are you asking officially or unofficially?' Roxana parried.

He laughed.

'I beg you not to be suspicious of me. Now that you have shown me your sculptures, you must know that I am prepared to insist that you should remain in Bali for ever, if it is your wish to do so.'

'Do you really mean that?'

'I am not speaking lightly, but as one connoisseur of beauty to another.'

'Is that what you think I am?'

'It is what I know you are,' the Count replied. 'The difference between us lies in the fact that, while I can only collect—you create!'

'I think that is the nicest compliment I have ever received!' Roxana said.

'I can think of a great many others I would like to pay you,' he replied.

She looked at him with a question in her eyes, and he knew suddenly that she was afraid he might be difficult as he was sure the Governor was being.

Before he could speak, before he could think of how to reassure her, a woman walked across the court-yard and stepped up onto the floor on which they were sitting.

She was a middle-aged woman with the air of respectability and authority of a senior servant.

Her grey hair was covered by the white linen cap that was worn in Holland by the women who served the Count in his houses as they had served his father and mother.

118

Geertruida put down the tray she carried in her hand, and with a respectful curtsey said:

'I hope, *Mijnheer*, the fruit juice is to your liking.'

'*Goede morgan*,' the Count said and continued in Dutch. 'I have heard from your mistress how much she relies on you to look after her and protect her. It is a task I feel you perform most conscientiously.'

'I do my best, *Mijnheer*, but it is not always easy in a strange land.'

'I appreciate your difficulties, and I hope I will be able to make things easier for you.'

'Thank you, *Mijnheer*.'

Geertruida curtsied again and withdrew.

When she was out of ear-shot Roxana said:

'That was very kind of you. His Excellency is always rude to Geertruida and she resents it.'

'Why should he be rude?' the Count asked.

Again he saw the colour come into Roxana's cheeks and realised she wished she had not spoken.

After a moment he said:

'I asked you to tell me why he should be rude.'

'I have...told him that Geertruida is my...Chaperon, and he...thinks she is... listening to what he is saying to me.'

'Would you like me to speak to him?' the Count asked after a moment.

Roxana gave a little cry.

'No...no...of course not! Please...forget that I said that...it was...stupid and indiscreet of me.'

'Why should you be afraid of him?'

'He could...send me away. He could make me...leave Bali.'

'Do you really think he would do that?'

'He might do so...'

The Count was aware that the end of the sentence might have been: '...unless I do what he says.'

He felt a sudden surge of anger.

It was intolerable that the Governor, who he thought was an uncouth, boorish type of man, should persecute anything so delicate and sensitive as Roxana.

She had risen to pour out a glass of fruit juice and set it in front of him.

He looked up at her and asked:

'What can I do to help you?'

'You can say that you consider it important for me to remain here so that I can go on with my wood-carving.'

'I will do that, of course, but what will happen when I have left?'

She shrugged her shoulders and made what he thought was a pathetic little gesture with her hand.

'It will be easier,' she said in a voice he could hardly hear, 'when Meviouw van Kaerstock returns from Holland.'

The Count's lips tightened. He realised there was nothing much he could do, and to show his partisanship for this English girl now might make it very much more difficult for her after he had left.

As if she knew what he was thinking Roxana said:

'Please do not worry over me. All I want is to be...forgotten and...ignored.'

'I think that would be impossible wherever you might be.'

He felt again that she was shy of his compliment and sipped the delicious juice in which he recognised various native fruits.

Because he thought it wise to change the subject he said:

'I would like to visit your teacher. What is his name?'

He spoke casually and was not prepared for the sudden look of fear he saw in Roxana's eyes.

'It is not...easy to get there,' she answered. 'He lives high up in the forest. It is...a sharp climb.'

The Count thought that as she spoke she realised how young and athletic he was and added quickly:

'Besides, Ida Anak Temu does not like visitors, especially when they are...Dutch!'

The Count noted the name in some methodical part of his brain. Aloud he said:

'The Governor assures me there is no resentment or rebellion amongst the Balinese.'

'They would not dare to show it openly,' Roxana flashed.

'But it is there all the same!'

'Of course it is there!' she answered.

'You sound as if you too think they should have been left to their own devices.'

He saw that she debated with herself whether she should tell the truth. Then she said:

'The Balinese are a very happy people and before the Dutch came they had achieved a remarkable civilisation.'

She looked at the Count to see if he was about to contradict her and went on:

'Their religion binds them together by ideals and harmonious thought. They are closely united in the worship of their wonderful ancestral gods.'

'A strange statement from a Christian in the house of a Missionary,' the Count remarked dryly.

'I am not a Missionary,' Roxana retorted, 'and I hate what the Dutch are trying to do to people who are truly noble and intrinsically good if only they are left to themselves. Everything in the Balinese faith is against what is wrong and evil. Can Christianity teach them anything better than that?'

'I agree with you,' the Count said, 'but it still surprises me that you should speak in the way you do.'

'I try to keep silent,' Roxana said, 'but sometimes the insufferable stupidity and the limited outlook of the Dutch makes me furious!'

The Count laughed, then said:

'I can only beg of you to be careful what you say in front of the type of my countrymen whom I met at dinner last night. They are very bigoted, and I can understand that they think of you as an incendiary force which could disturb their peace of mind.'

'I only wish I could make them realise the harm they are doing to these simple people,' Roxana said.

'Do you fight this crusade all on your own?' he enquired.

'I think I have...unseen resources on my side,' she answered.

'I am sure of that,' he replied quietly. 'At the same time, be careful.'

She gave a little sigh.

'It is what I try to be and Geertruida admonishes me every morning to guard my tongue.'

'Geertruida is right,' the Count answered, 'and I feel sure that she thinks it is time that I left here, unless we are to have the whole village gossiping about you.'

'It is not the village that will gossip,' Roxana answered, 'but the Dutch! I think sometimes I hate them with their suspicious minds.'

Again she realised that she had said too much and glanced at him quickly in case he should be angry.

'Shall I answer what you are thinking?' he enquired, 'by telling you that anything we say to each other in private will not be repeated? Not by me, at any rate.'

'Thank you,' Roxana said. 'I do not mean to be indiscreet, but I get carried away.'

'In a very charming manner!'

'Perhaps it is because I have no-one to talk to,' she went on as if she was following the train of her thoughts, 'except for Geertruida, and she, much as I love her, has a very conventional outlook.'

'And quite right!' the Count said approvingly. 'But because I feel I am pehaps supplying a need in your existence, may I come again?'

'I would like you to,' she said, 'and will you please accept as a gift the goddess you admired? I would like to think she will look after and protect you.'

She saw the expression on the Count's face and added:

'She has a very special and powerful magic of her own, I assure you!'

The Count threw out his hands.

'In this country I am prepared to believe in anything, even in magic!'

'If you live here long enough,' Roxana answered, 'you will not only believe, but you will see it...happen.'

There was a note in her voice which told him something he had half-suspected.

'You believe it was magic that killed your uncle?'

Roxana nodded.

'The *Pedanda* had, I discovered, told the people that he was a *Leyek*. After that he had no chance.'

The Count thought that a week ago he would have laughed such a statement to scorn. Now he was not sure.

There was something in the very air of Bali that hinted at mysteries, something in the Temples that he had passed while riding towards the village which aroused strange feelings he did not understand himself.

He felt now as if Roxana was hardly human.

How could she be anything but mystical when she could see a form in a block of wood and carve an expression of ecstasy that he had seen before only in pictures by the great Italian Masters?

He reached out and took her hand.

'I have come to Bali to find out many things about its people,' he said. 'If I promise to do nothing to hurt them, but perhaps to make things better for them, will you trust me?'

He felt her fingers quiver in his. Then as he looked into her eyes they were both very still.

'I did not...expect to do...so,' she answered in a low voice, 'but...I do...trust you.'

★ ★ ★ ★

Riding home the Count felt that Roxana had given him a lot to think about.

At the same time, he could not help feeling the life she was living alone except for the old servant made her very vulnerable.

It seemed absurd on such short acquaintance, but he found himself worrying over the Governor's attitude towards her and over the Dutch women who were antagonistic to her.

Because she was, as far as he knew, the only English person on the island there was, he thought, no-one to whom she could turn in trouble.

It was ridiculous to think for a moment that she could look after herself.

No woman who was as beautiful as she was would be able to prevent herself from being pursued by every man who saw her.

The Count had only to think of the thick figure and red face of the Governor to know that he would not hesitate to use every weapon in his power to make Roxana subservient to his will.

She was already afraid of him, and he had only to remember the anger that the Governor had been unable to conceal when he had decided to visit her alone, to know what His Excellency felt.

The Count was not used to being perturbed by other people's feelings.

There were, of course, innumerable problems in his life, but they were mostly ones of State, protocol and of love.

He could not remember when he had ever before felt he wanted to protect and help a woman who was not directly involved in his own life.

But then, he told himself, he could never remember meeting anyone quite like Roxana.

He admitted that she attracted him, but, again, in a different way from other women.

He did not want to flirt with her, he did not even at the moment desire her in the acknowledged sense of the word.

Instead he wanted to understand her, he wanted to know more about what she thought and felt.

He wanted more than anything to realise how she could carve as she did and have the inspiration that he had never expected to find in one of her sex.

Yet when he reached Government House, the Count was almost questioning whether

Roxana's carvings were really as brilliant as he had thought them to be.

It was as if his mind could not acknowledge that such talent was possible, while something deeper, some unpredictable instinct told him she had a genius that he must acknowledge.

It was almost luncheon-time by the time he reached the house, and when he had washed and changed he walked into the big Reception-Room to find the Governor waiting for him, a glass in his hand.

'I hope, Count, you enjoyed yourself.'

His tone of voice was unmistakably hostile and the Count replied quietly:

'I found Miss Barclay's work very interesting. I must admit however I have not had much experience of wood-carving.'

'You will find a surfeit of it in Bali.'

'So I believe.'

A servant offered the Count a drink and when he accepted it and was sitting looking out over the colourful garden the Governor said, almost as if the words were forced from him:

'What did the girl tell you?'

'About what?'

'Her life here—the people—the way she is treated.'

'We spoke mostly of her carving. I think she should definitely be allowed to continue with her lessons.'

'So, she has persuaded you to plead for her for an extension of her stay?'

'I certainly think her talent should not be wasted, but I presume there are other places where she could find a teacher, if it is impracticable for her to stay here.'

The Count spoke indifferently and he knew that this attitude had the desired effect on the Governor.

'I try to be lenient,' he said, 'but I can assure you in this place it is difficult to please everyone.'

'I am sure it is,' the Count answered, 'and justice, I am told, can have two sides to it.'

'You are right! Of course you are right!' the Governor said in an over-hearty manner.

He threw himself down in a chair beside the Count, his legs out-stretched.

'The trouble with this damned place,' he said, 'is that there is very little to amuse one, unless of course one has a partiality for the Balinese women.'

★ ★ ★ ★

As soon as the Count was out of sight Roxana ran into the kitchen where Geertruida was preparing the meal.

'It is all right! It is all right!' she cried excitedly. 'The Count is going to help me and there is no need for us to be afraid that he will insist on our leaving the island!'

She thought that Geertruida looked disbelieving and went on:

'He understood! He actually understood, Geertruida, what I am trying to portray. He obviously knows a lot about sculpture.'

'I heard of him when we were in Holland,' Geertruida said. 'He's very rich, related to the Queen Dowager, and has more love-affairs in a month than I can count on my fingers!'

The way she spoke made Roxana suddenly silent.

She looked at her in perplexity.

'You do not...like the Count, Geertruida?'

'He's too plausible and too good-looking!'

Roxana laughed.

'You can hardly hold his looks against him!'

'They say it gets him everything he wants!' Geertruida retorted.

'And as he wants to help us why should we complain?' Roxana asked. 'He has promised me that he will try to influence the Governor to let us stay. That is all that matters.'

'He'll be coming again?' Geertruida asked suspiciously.

'I...I am sure he has a lot of...other things to see to and a long list of...people to meet,' Roxana replied evasively.

'Now listen to me, Miss Roxana,' Geertruida said. 'We've enough trouble with the

Governor coming sniffing around here every moment of the day without having the Count as well! You don't want to trust him!'

'Why do you say that?'

'Because if he discovers Karel's existence, like all the rest he'll push him into an Orphanage because he's Dutch and nothing you could say would make the slightest difference!'

Roxana made a half-stifled protest and Geertruida went on:

'You are English, Miss, and don't forget it! The Dutch listen to no-one but themselves. They obey their own laws, and the Count is no different from the rest. You mark my words!'

Geertruida finished by slapping what she was holding in her hands down on the table.

Then she found she was talking to nobody for Roxana had wandered away.

Geertruida could see her white gown under the shadows of the palm-thatch of her Studio.

She was touching the head of the kneeling girl where the Count had touched it.

Almost irresistibly her fingers went to the thrown-back neck, moving slowly, gently over the smoothness of the wood.

CHAPTER FOUR

Roxana was working at her carving of the man's torso when she heard the sound of a horse coming into the court-yard.

She did not turn her head because she was certain who her visitor was, and a few minutes later the Count came to stand beside her.

It was very hot and she was wearing the thinnest of her gowns. Her skin glowed through the fine material and there was a flush on her face.

She did not raise her eyes, but after a moment as the Count did not speak she said:

'You are early this morning.'

'I came to ask your help.'

'My...help?'

Roxana was so surprised that she stopped

work to stand staring at him.

He was wearing only a shirt with his riding-breeches and the thought came to her that his body resembled that of the figure she was carving.

Because it seemed so intimate to compare them she felt shy and she half-turned her face away to say:

'I cannot think I heard you...aright. How could I...help you?'

The Count did not answer the question but said:

'Did you have a model for this?'

He put his hand as he spoke on the wooden head of the figure.

'No,' Roxana replied. 'He was there in my mind as soon as the piece of wood was brought to me.'

She smiled and added:

'I have something to show you.'

She moved across her Studio to where at the far end the Count saw several new large pieces of wood had been placed.

One was tall and strangely fashioned so

that the branches which had been lopped off at the top seemed to twine above the main trunk.

He felt that Roxana was testing him to see if his vision of what the wood should become was the same as hers.

He stood looking at it, forcing himself to concentrate and for the moment to forget Roxana, who had seemed when he saw her at work, to look even lovelier than she had before.

Her hair with its russet hue seemed to glow against the coconut matting which obscured the sun, and yet it appeared to glow with light in a manner which fascinated him.

'What do you see?' Roxana asked and brought his mind back to the wood in front of him.

Unexpectedly he laughed.

'I am afraid to make a mistake and show my ignorance.'

'I would not like you to do that.'

'Then what do you see?' he enquired.

'To me it is very obvious that there are two people entwined together, their heads close; perhaps they are kissing, but that, as you know, is a very un-Balinese custom.'

As soon as she had spoken she knew he saw as if through her eyes what the wood held.

It was so clear, the man with his arms around the woman, holding her against his heart, their bodies pressed to each other. Even the curves of their heads, one higher than the other, were now visible.

He felt there was some magic in the way that Roxana was making him see what she herself saw with an inner eye.

Almost as if he resented her momentary superiority over him he said:

'If we were in Holland I would say that you were hypnotising me, but here in Bali...'

He paused for words.

'You are merely seeing with...your spirit, or your soul,' Roxana finished.

'You frighten me,' he protested, 'and yet I have to ask for your help.'

'In what way.'

He paused for a moment. Then he said:

'When I came to Bali against my will and, if I am truthful, very sceptical of what I would find here, I still told myself that I would try to understand its people and their ways.'

'It is right for you to feel like this.'

'But I realise that living at Government House it is very difficult to do so,' the Count went on. 'I have in fact escaped this morning by the simple method of leaving before the Governor came down to breakfast.'

'He will be very angry,' Roxana warned.

'That does not perturb me,' the Count replied loftily. 'At the same time, I am beginning to realise that if I am to spend my time looking at Dutch buildings, meeting Dutch people, and seeing plans for improvements which I doubt will ever be put into operation, I might just as well have stayed at home!'

To himself the Count admitted that was

not possible, for he had been forced to visit Bali, whether he wished it or not.

At the same time he knew he was now intrigued by the country, by its people and by Roxana. He had therefore, no intention of being continually circumvented in everything he wished to do by the Governor.

'How can I help you?' Roxana asked.

'His Excellency is trying to persuade me to watch cock-fighting, a sport which has never interested me, to attend bullock races, which I understand may take place some time this month, and also to watch the—dancing girls.'

The way he said the last two words made Roxana glance at him sharply.

'He is ordering them to come to Government House,' he finished.

'Then that will certainly not be the real dancing which should take place in its proper environment.'

'That is what I thought,' the Count answered.

He did not tell Roxana that he knew the

Governor was envisaging the type of girl who would obey his command and would be ready to amuse them in a different way after the dancing was over.

The Count was very fastidious and he had never, although few people would have believed it, made love to a woman unless he was actually attracted by her.

Even in Paris where he had spent a great deal of his time he never frequented the "Houses of Pleasure" as most of his contemporaries did.

Anything of that sort he did not find amusing, and the women to whom he made love were either of his own class or were stars of the stage or ballet.

He was not prepared to criticise the Governor for finding his amusement while his wife was away with the lovely and graceful Balinese women, but that was not the type of entertainment that he found attractive.

Also he was determined to see the dancing that was genuine and not a show put on for the purposes of gain.

He had read in the books he had studied that the *Lelong* dancing was the distillation of the perfection of human movement and was performed only by girls who had not reached puberty.

This, he learned, gave it an abstract purity that was not to be found anywhere else in the world.

The *Topeng* historical mask-plays were generally danced by older men who, by changing their masks, impersonated brave Kings, scheming Princes, foolish Prime Ministers and warriors.

There were also, he knew, Temple dances, although he thought it unlikely that as a foreigner he would be able to view those.

He saw that Roxana was thinking, then suddenly she clapped her hands.

The small girl who had waited on them before came running from what the Count suspected was the kitchen-quarters.

Roxana spoke to her in slow but intelligible Balinese. When the child understood what was asked of her she went running across the

144

court-yard and out through the gate-way.

'I hope we shall have the answer to your question in a few minutes,' Roxana said to the Count. 'In the meantime, I think I should go on with my work.'

'Why the hurry?' he enquired.

She seemed to puzzle for a second over his question, then she answered:

'I have a feeling of urgency, as if unless I work now I shall never finish it. It is… something I cannot explain, and yet it is… there.'

'I think you are just being mysterious to make me curious.'

He knew as he spoke teasingly that such an idea had never entered Roxana's head.

As if such a suggestion was too foolish to be answered she merely ignored it and, picking up her chisel and hammer, went back to the work she had been doing when he arrived.

He found a wicker-seated chair and seated himself on it, astride, as if he was on a horse, his arms resting on the high back.

He watched her and wondered if any woman of any nationality could be more graceful and at the same time so lovely.

He was certain now of her resemblance to his statue of Aphrodite which, when he had bought it, had been lying for hundreds of years in the sea. It had given the marble a softness like real flesh.

He thought now that if the head had still been there the face would have been Roxana's.

She straightened herself to look at him.

'You are making me...nervous.'

'Why?'

'Because I feel you are...thinking of me.'

'Why should that make you nervous?'

She hesitated a moment, then she said:

'Perhaps I am afraid of your criticism.'

He knew that that was not the truth and that she had sensed that he was thinking something very different.

He would have answered, but at that moment the small girl came back into the court-yard and with her was a middle-aged man wearing only a *sarong* round his hips.

Roxana stepped down from the high floor to greet him and they talked for a few minutes. The Count watched the sunshine glitter on her hair and the gestures of her slim hands as emphasised what she was trying to say.

Finally she turned back towards him and she was smiling.

'I have good news!'

The Count rose to his feet and she made a little gesture with her hands towards the man standing in the court-yard.

'This is Ponok,' she said, 'and although it will not be easy he has promised to take us to-night to see the *Ketjak*.'

'It is a dance?' the Count asked.

'It is the wildest and most dramatic of all the Balinese dances,' Roxana explained. 'But it only takes place at night and we have to travel some distance into the forest.'

She looked at the Count a little anxiously as she said:

'I am afraid there is no way of getting there

except by walking.'

There was an apologetic note in her voice and the Count replied:

'Are you suggesting it might be too far and too exhausting for me?'

'It is not that,' Roxana answered, 'but you might be...too grand.'

He laughed.

'I assure you I am a very humble pilgrim at the fount of knowledge wherever I can find it!'

'Then can you manage to be here soon after four-thirty?' Roxana asked.

The Count was not surprised at the early hour.

He knew that as Bali was not far from the Equator dusk came about five o'clock, the shadows lengthened by five-thirty until the brilliant flowers, and the golden stones of the Temples merged into a misty grey.

'I will be here!' he said firmly, 'and I am grateful. Will you tell this man how grateful I am?'

Roxana translated his wishes into Balinese

and Ponok bowed with the dignity that was characteristic of his race.

'Should I give him some money?' the Count asked Roxana in a low voice.

She shook her head decisively.

'Certainly not!' she said. 'He takes us as a favour to me. It would be impossible to buy his services.'

She saw the surprise on the Count's face and added:

'I will reciprocate his friendliness tomorrow or the next day by giving him one of my small carvings.'

'That, I am convinced,' the Count said, 'far outweighs the values of anything that could be bought.'

He made a gesture towards the boy who was holding his horse and when he brought the animal towards him, he said:

'I am going to leave you, although I am very reluctant to do so. I will take part in the excruciatingly boring programme which the Governor has planned for me, but I assure you I shall be here by four-thirty and nothing will prevent me!'

'I will have some refreshment for you before we start,' Roxana promised.

'It still sounds as if you are afraid I will faint by the wayside,' the Count replied.

'Watching the *Ketjak* is quite tiring and quite different from attending the Opera or a performance of *Les Sylphides*.'

As the Count rode away he thought irritably that she was classifying him with the type of man who would expect the best box, the most comfortable seats, to be available for him at every entertainment.

He knew at the same time, that he was looking forward to this evening with the eagerness of a schoolboy attending his first play.

★ ★ ★ ★

It was dark long before Roxana and the Count reached what seemed to him to be the centre of the forest.

In the magical dusk they had seen farmers

trudging homewards from the darkening *Sawahs*, their hoes over their shoulders, their legs stained by mud.

They passed through small villages where smoke from the cooking-fires was blue against the shadows of the trees and the burnt-orange walls.

The air seemed at moments to be filled with a flight of myriad dragonflies, then at last after a long walk, they came unexpectedly to where in a clearing a large number of villagers were crouching in a circle around a fire.

As they followed Ponok, who marched ahead of them carrying a small candle-lantern that he did not light until darkness actually fell, Roxana in a soft, low voice explained the *Ketjak* to the Count.

'It is called ''The Monkey Dance'',' she said, 'because Garuda, the symbolic bird of Vishna, is helped by Hanuman and his army of monkeys to free Prince Rama and the Princess Sita who has been abducted by the King of the Demons.'

The Count was listening with only half his mind to the story, while finding himself instead moved by Roxana's voice.

It had a musical quality that seemed particularly soft and magical in the shadows of the great trees and with the fragrance of the forest all around them.

'Originally the *Ketjak* was performed by villagers,' she went on, 'when an epidemic ravaged their herds. It was supposed to drive away evil spirits.'

'And to-day?' the Count asked.

'There is usually some specific reason why the *Ketjak* should take place: perhaps someone believes that he is haunted by a *Leyak* or that a witch who is called Rangda has placed a curse upon him.'

'And you think the *Ketjak* will be effective in such instances?' the Count asked.

Roxana thought he was laughing at her and she glanced at him questioningly before she replied:

'I think faith...wherever one finds it...can work...miracles!'

152

It was the perfect answer, the Count thought, but how many women of his acquaintance could have made it?

Ponok took them to the outside of the circle of people crouching around the fire.

The Count saw there was an empty space left in the middle where he guessed the characters of the drama would appear.

Then as they waited he tried to see what was happening around him.

More and more men appeared, and with them lights began to glow in which he could see everything more clearly.

There were only wicks in coconut-oil and a few lanterns. Then the flames of the fire leapt and there was a complete and absolute silence.

It was almost as if everyone held his breath, and the Count felt as if the waiting was so poignant that it was almost unbearable.

There was a loud clap so unexpected that it jerked him upright. Then from outside the circle of flickering wicks and the tightly-packed half-naked bodies of the men came the first incantation of a singer, a hollow, rolling call, not unlike the prayer from a Minaret.

It ended in a massive hiss like escaping steam which increased in volume until it became a roaring challenge, then merged into a slow chant.

The chorus broke into the *Ketjak*, a harsh, gabbling, chattering staccato, sharp and chilling.

The men bent forward and stretched out their arms and their voices seemed to become a pattern of hoots, shouts, groans and hisses that ended with a throaty *"heeeeee"* which seemed to hit one in the stomach.

From then on the Count felt as if it had become part of the drama itself.

He was Prince Rama in a glittering costume, mad with despair, in search of his lost wife.

He felt that he himself took part in the fight in which a demon let fly an arrow which turned into a serpent and encircled the Prince.

But the gods came to his rescue and Hanuman and his monkeys succeeded in freeing the Prince and giving him back his Consort, the Princess Sita.

But it was the chorus of male voices which, with no instrumental music to accompany them, reached chilling peaks when the Count felt his skin shudder and tingle.

Then they descended to even more frightening depths while the rustle and click of their fingers made the tension almost intolerable.

He felt he was mesmerised by the nightmare movement of their bodies, by their arms casting flickering and magical shadows as all the time a hundred-and-fifty voices seemed to stab the darkness of the night and into the very heart of those who listened.

When finally it was over, the men slumped forward in a state of exhaustion like, the Count thought, oarsmen after a long gruelling race.

He knew that he himself also felt physically exhausted, and yet mentally exhilarated as he had never been in his life before.

He had been lifted out of himself and he knew as he came back to earth that Roxana felt the same as he did.

For some minutes it was impossible to move. They could only sit breathing deeply as if they had swum against a violent sea and had only just arrived.

Then Ponok rose to his feet and the Count put out his hand to help Roxana to hers.

As he touched her he felt as if a spark from the flames burnt through his whole body uniting with the flame in hers.

Their eyes met and after a second she said with lips which found it difficult to speak:

'Y...you...understood?'

He nodded.

For the moment he seemed to have lost the power of speech.

Then still holding hands they followed Ponok's lantern through the silent crowds that were dispersing into the shadows.

They seemed somehow to have no more

substance or humanity than the densest part of the forest itself.

They walked for some way before the Count said:

'If I had not seen that with my own eyes or heard it with my own ears I should never have believed such a thing was possible!'

'I hoped that was what you would say,' Roxana replied.

His fingers tightened on hers as he asked:

'Would you have brought me if you had known I would not have felt like this?'

'No!'

'How did you know it would have such an effect on me?'

'I just knew it,' she said simply.

'Such a thing has never happened to me before,' the Count said. 'Now you have opened a door, Roxana, which I think it will be difficult to close.'

'Do you want to close it?'

'No! At the same time it will mean mental adjustment.'

'I think the word should be...development,' she answered.

'Yes, of course,' he agreed.

They walked on in silence, and yet the Count thought they were talking to each other without words, saying things that he had never expressed to himself, let alone to another person.

When they emerged from the forest the stars and the moon lit the rice fields which lay between them and the village where Roxana lived.

Mysteriously blue, filled with vibrations that he could sense, the Count thought he had stepped into an enchanted world of such beauty that there were no words to describe it.

Then as they walked on he saw across the fields lights that seemed more brilliant and more profuse than one would have expected from the oil-lamps of a few small houses.

'What is happening there?' he enquired.

'I think it is a festival or a feast,' Roxana replied. 'Every village has special things to celebrate, and they will be dancing and making offerings to the gods especially if a marriage has taken place.'

The Count ceased walking.

'Could we go and see?' he asked.

It was not only that he wanted to look at what was taking place, but he had a desire for the evening not to come to an end, not to reach too quickly Roxana's house where he must leave her.

She spoke to Ponok and the man seemed to consider for a moment whether they would be unwelcome in a small village.

Then he decided they could go there and Roxana, drawing the Count by the hand, turned towards the lights.

It took them only a short time to walk across the soft ground to reach the village.

The entrance to it was decorated with streamers and flowers, and when they entered they saw the main shrine was piled with the gifts that had been brought there all day by the women who had carried them on their heads.

Everything was in the brilliant colours of

the carvings but now the pink, blue, green and yellow was supplied by the food and fruit.

The rice *satis* and salt had been blessed by the priest but there was sea turtle and *get-jok* or minced turtle-flesh with grated coconut, and suckling pig ready for the spit, besides chickens so thin and long-legged they were nick-named "racing birds".

It was all very simple, and yet beautiful in its own way. The villagers were seated in a circle watching a little girl of twelve or thirteen years old, clad in brocade down to her feet and wearing a flowered tiara on her head.

The musicians were playing for her to move backwards and forwards in the strange dance that is performed with a completely expressionless face.

She moved her chin from right to left and the upper part of her face was motionless. Only her eyes seemed to roll in their sockets darting from one corner to another with extraordinary rapidity.

Standing in the background the Count and Roxana watched for some time. Then without speaking for fear of disturbing the spectators, Roxana drew the Count back through the gateway and out into the quiet night.

'I would have rather liked to stay until the end,' he said almost resentfully.

'That is a *Lelong*,' Roxana replied, 'and it can go on for five hours.'

'Five hours!' he exclaimed.

She gave a little laugh at his surprise.

'There is never any hurry in Bali.'

'But you are hurrying me home,' he complained.

'I am thinking of Ponok,' she replied. 'The Balinese hate the dark. If he were alone and not accompanying us, he would be singing and shouting at the top of his voice.'

The Count smiled.

'I know why, to keep away evil spirits!'

'You are beginning to learn,' Roxana said. 'Darkness is full of the unknown and that is why they love the light and the sun, and have no wish to encounter a *Leyek* who only

161

operates at night.'

They walked on, still holding hands, and after what the Count thought was a regrettably short time they reached the village.

He had left his horse in charge of the usual small boy in the court-yard and although the walls were high there was a faint light above them and he guessed that Geertruida would be waiting for their return.

Outside the gate-way Ponok stopped, and when Roxana thanked him he bowed and walked away towards his own house which was in the village itself.

As Ponok left, Roxana would have entered the gate-way of her house, but the Count drew her to one side beneath the branches of a frangipani tree the fragrance of its scent on the air.

When Ponok's footsteps had died away in the distance there was only silence, the stars overhead and the moonlight which revealed Roxana's face as she lifted it towards the Count's enquiringly.

'What is it?' she asked, as if she thought

he had something special to say to her.

'I have to thank you for an enchanting evening,' he replied.

'Was it really enchanting?'

'That is not really the right word because there is nothing in my vocabulary to express what you have given me.'

'I am glad it...pleased you.'

The Count smiled.

' "Pleased" is not very expressive,' he said, 'but it will have to do.'

Roxana waited.

He had not released her hand, and now she felt herself waiting as she had waited for the *Ketjak* with a feeling that seemed to grow in intensity.

'I cannot thank you in words,' the Count said, 'so I will do it another way.'

He put his arms round her as he spoke and drew her close against him.

She did not resist him, then his mouth was on hers and he held her captive.

For a moment his kiss was very gentle, almost as if he was still caught up in the exaltation of the *Ketjak* and the magical beauty of the rice fields.

Then the softness of her lips and a feeling of spiritual intensity that he had never known before made his mouth become more insistent, more demanding.

It was not only a physical passion that was rising within him, it was something far deeper, more fundamental.

It was part of the emotion that had been evoked by the dancers and part too of a sacred force within himself that had never been aroused before.

He wanted Roxana, he wanted her in a manner in which a man may yearn for the divine and yet know that it is within himself.

His whole being reached out towards her and he knew as he held her in his arms that she was a part of him and they were invisible.

To Roxana similarly the Count was the moonlight, the stars, the land she loved, and the people who had crept into her heart.

She felt that she could see through his

body, as she could see through a piece of wood, to what lay inside.

And what she saw there was not only him but herself, and everything in which she believed and had tried to attain.

It was like coming home and finding that the past and the future were one and had become the present so vivid, so vibrant, that the sensation and emotion of love needed no explanation.

As the Count kissed her she knew that everything that was magic in Bali was in that kiss, and the mysteries they had watched together had brought them to the point where they need no longer pretend but could recognise each other across time.

When finally the Count raised his head to look down at her, she saw that he was enveloped with light, the light which guided her in her carving, in her thoughts and in her dreams.

'I...love you!'

Those three words had been said to the Count on many occasions and yet he thought he heard them now for the first time.

'How can I have found you here, of all places?' he asked.

'I have been...waiting for you,' she murmured, 'and it would not matter where...but here it is more...perfect than anywhere else.'

'Of course,' he answered. ' ''The Island of Paradise''—''The Island of Gods''!'

'They have blessed us,' Roxana whispered, 'and to-night I want to believe that the *Ketjak* has driven away all the evil.'

'I will protect you from everything,' he answered, but he was thinking not of the demons and the *Leyek* but of the Governor.

He kissed her again and time stood still.

★ ★ ★ ★

It might have been an hour or a century that passed before the barking of a dog in the village disturbed them and brought them back to reality.

'I...must go!'

The words were almost a paean of wonder

and ecstasy: Roxana's voice was not her own but the music of the spheres and the movement of the blossom above their heads.

'My darling, my sweet! How could I know there was anyone like you in the whole world?'

The Count's fingers touched her cheek as he spoke, then the softness of her neck, as he had touched the carving of the girl in prayer.

He had known her skin would be like the petals of a flower, and yet he knew there was a strength in her body and in her spirit that had nothing soft or limp about it.

He smoothed back the hair from her forehead, then looking into her eyes said:

'Go now, my precious. I shall see you tomorrow, but I am not certain at what time.'

'You know...I will be waiting,' Roxana answered.

Then as if she understood that neither of them could bear the anti-climax of saying good-bye in the court-yard in front of the boy who was minding the Count's horse, she slipped from his arms and through the gate-way, and he was alone.

He waited for some minutes, conscious that his heart was still beating strangely in his breast and that he was feeling different in every way from what he had ever felt before when he loved a woman.

This was love, he told himself, that he had never dreamt existed; a love that could not be compared for one moment with the desire or infatuation that had held him for a short time at many a woman's side before inevitably he grew bored and had no further use for her.

He told himself he was like a pilgrim moving relentlessly on a path that he sensed would carry him to real love, but which twisted and turned so that he had trodden many false paths before he found the right one.

He looked back and regretted that he had wasted so much time and that many women had been hurt in his fruitless search for perfection which had eluded him.

He thought of Luise van Heydberg and was ashamed. How could he have been so foolish, so obtuse, as to have become involved with such a woman?

Just for a moment because of his feeling for Roxana he was afraid.

Afraid that he might be punished for the sins he had committed in the past. Afraid he might lose her; for that would be a punishment he deserved.

Then he told himself he was being absurd.

The fight between good and evil which he had seen in the *Ketjak* was still lingering in his mind.

Quickly, deliberately, he walked through the gate-way to find as he expected that the bamboo screens were closed and there was no sign of Roxana. Only the boy and the horse were waiting for him.

He gave the boy a coin that made him stare at it in astonishment. Then without speaking, the Count mounted and rode through the gate-way.

Outside he glanced for a moment at the

frangipani tree under which he had kissed Roxana and thought the magic was still there, almost like a blue light illuminating the shadows.

Then, conscious of the singing within his heart, he rode on through the sleeping village towards Government House.

★ ★ ★ ★

Roxana awoke in the morning with a feeling of happiness that made her think the sunshine flooding her small room was more brilliant than she had ever known it before.

How could it be possible, she asked herself, that she could fall in love so quickly and so completely that the whole world seemed filled with love and that her body vibrated as if to the music of angels?

She had always thought that one day she would find a man whom she would love and who would love her and, as in the fairy-stories she had read as a child, she would live happily ever afterwards.

But how could she have imagined that of all places she would find him in Bali and that he would in fact be Dutch?

She had disliked the Dutch so fervently ever since she came to live with her aunt and uncle that she had believed it impossible even to have a close friend amongst them.

Her prejudice was, in fact, due to the way her uncle was condescended to and looked down upon by the Dutch in Holland, and held in contempt by the Dutch who had settled in Bali.

It was because she despised their snobbery that Roxana had vowed to herself that she would never use her social position to ease her path amongst them.

She had, in fact, as she had told the Count, wanted only that they should ignore her and leave her alone.

To be entertained by anyone because of her antecedents rather than for herself would be, for her, an intolerable insult, especially if it came from the Dutch.

But now amazingly, unbelievably, she was

in love with a Dutchman, and she knew that where love was concerned, just as there were no boundaries they could not cross, it would be impossible for their different nationalities to be of any importance.

'I love him!' she told the sunshine. 'I love him so much that he fills my mind and my heart and my whole body to the exclusion of everything else!'

She knew that all she wanted was for the hours to pass quickly until he could be with her again and, although it was still very early, she rose feeling somehow that she would be nearer to him if she was working in her Studio.

He understood, he knew what she was trying to portray by her carving, and she was sure that last night, even before he had kissed her, the emotions they had shared in watching the *Ketjak* had drawn them closer still.

But now Roxana could feel the Count's lips still on hers and she could re-capture the ecstasy that had blazed like flame through her body and which had lifted her mind up into the sky.

'How could anything else be of importance?' she asked, and suddenly remembered Karel.

Just for a moment she felt as if a cold wind touched her.

Would the Count understand? she wondered. Would he be prepared for her sake to evade the Dutch ruling regarding orphans and take Karel out of the country?

It would not be easy, she thought, but surely not impossible.

She told herself that when he came to her she would tell him frankly what she was hiding and was sure he would understand.

When she was dressed, she was just about to leave her room when Geertruida came in with a small glass of fruit juice that she always brought her in the morning.

'You are up already!' she exclaimed needlessly. 'What is the hurry?'

'I was awake,' Roxana answered.

With the light in her eyes which seemed

like the sunshine itself she said:

'Oh, Geertruida, I had such a wonderful evening!'

The maid looked at her, then asked sharply:

'What happened?'

'I am in love!' Roxana said. 'And love is more perfect, more marvellous, more completely and utterly divine than I ever imagined it could be!'

Geertruida's lips tightened. Then she asked slowly and in a voice that sounded somehow ominous:

'Has he asked you to marry him?'

'There was no time to talk,' Roxana replied in a low voice. 'He is coming to-day, then everything will be simple. I will tell him about Karel and he will take us all away back to Holland...to England...it does not matter where as long as we are together.'

'How can you be sure that is what he will do?' Geertruida enquired.

'I know everything about him,' Roxana said in a dreamy voice. 'We feel the same...

we think the same...we are the same!'

Geertruida put the fruit juice down on a table and there was an expression of darkness on her face, but she did not speak.

She only moved about picking up Roxana's nightgown from the floor and tidying the bed.

After a long time Roxana gave a deep sigh.

'I am so happy, Geertruida, I feel as if I am a bird soaring above the trees or a butterfly hovering over the flowers...I am happy as I have not been happy ever before in my whole life!'

'You must be sure!'

'Sure of what?'

'That the Count will understand when you tell him about Karel.'

'I know he will understand.'

'And suppose he does not? Suppose they take him away and put him in the Orphanage?'

'How could you think he would allow that? How can you imagine he would betray our love?'

'I am not saying he would,' Geertruida answered. 'I am only telling you to make sure.'

She paused before she said:

'You are old enough to decide what you want in your life, but Karel is helpless. There is no-one to care for him except you and me, Miss Roxana.'

'I will make sure before I tell the Count where Karel is,' Roxana said. 'He told me to trust him, and I do. This morning when he comes I shall trust him completely as I intend to do for the rest of my life.'

She walked, as she spoke, out of the bedroom and went towards her studio.

Left behind Geertruida clasped her hands together in prayer.

'Oh, God,' she said beneath her breath, in an anguished tone. 'Why did it have to be the Count van Haan, of all people?'

CHAPTER FIVE

Roxana worked all the morning, but there was no sign of the Count.

Geertruida prepared her a light meal about noon and then, when most people rested because the sun was so hot, Roxana went back to her carving.

She knew that for the first time she could not concentrate as she had always been able to do.

In fact, every nerve in her body was alert, waiting for the sound of an approaching horse, then to hear the Count's footsteps cross the court-yard.

Yet, at the same time, she knew she had never worked better because every mark of her chisel was made with love.

She stood for a long time looking at the

tree in which she had seen the figures of a man and a woman entwined.

She knew that while it was perhaps prophetic that it should have been brought to her at that particular time, she was sure that the clearness of her vision was due to what she felt inside herself.

That was how she and the Count had stood last night with his arms around her, his lips on hers, their bodies close to each other and their minds suffused with the light from the skies.

'How could I have known that love would be so beautiful?' she asked.

Then she thought she had, indeed, known.

Perhaps because the Count had loved her in another life it had given her an appreciation of beauty and an extra sense that made her feel, as other people were unable to do, that everything was part of a universal love.

Roxana had thought ever since she came to Bali that the gods, worshipped so fervently and with such devotion by the Balinese, were in reality the same as the God of the Christians, the Allah of the Mohammedans and the Buddha of the Buddhists.

How foolish it was, she had often thought, that men like her uncle, driven by an almost frantic desire to propagate their faith, must try to change people and take from them what had been deeply ingrained in their consciousness for generation after generation.

All religions which fought against evil must be good, and it was the way people lived and acted that was important, not the creed to which they paid lip-service.

Roxana felt as if everything the Balinese did, the closeness of their family life, the kindness they showed to each other, to children and to old people, was a living example of what religion should be.

They were far more holy, she told herself, than the Dutch with their social barriers and their intolerance of anyone who did not agree exactly with what they thought themselves.

She had thought that the Dutch had

certainly not learnt the secret of harmonious living.

During the two years she had been in Bali she had never seen a fight amongst either adults or children, while the people in the villages cared for each other and for those who were ill or in trouble in a manner that she had never found before in England or in Holland.

To-day, because she was so happy, Roxana did not want even to criticise the Dutch who ignored her uncle or Patrick Grenton who had driven her from England by marrying her mother.

'Because of the Count I love the whole world!' she thought.

Then her heart leapt because she heard someone enter the court-yard.

Because she was so excited at the thought of seeing the Count again, and yet at the same time a little shy because of the rapture and wonder of his kiss, she did not run towards him as she wanted to do.

Instead she remained with her back to him

continuing a little half-heartedly her work on the torso.

Then with a start she heard not his voice, but one she had learned to fear, say:

'I thought I should find you working when everyone else is asleep.'

She looked up to see the Governor, red-faced and over-powering, standing beside her and because she was surprised and had not expected him, it was impossible to move.

'I want to talk to you, Roxana.'

'About what?' she questioned.

'About your application to stay in Bali, for one thing.'

She knew he was trying to frighten her and because she had anticipated that was what he would say, she was not afraid.

'Your visitor, Count van Haan, thinks my work is important,' she said in a low voice without looking at him.

'The decision does not rest with the Count, who I understand will not be staying long,' the Governor replied, 'but with me!'

'Then I can only beg Your Excellency

to be generous.'

'That, as you well know, is what I am prepared to be, but like everyone else I have my price.'

There was silence for a moment. Then Roxana said:

'I have told you before that I have no wish to work in an office, nor, if I am to continue with my carving, would I have the time.'

'I appreciate that, and so I have another suggestion to make.'

Ordinary though the words were, they sounded somehow ominous and Roxana waited, knowing he intended to tell her what his suggestion was.

'It is not right that you should live here alone with only a servant,' the Governor said after a moment. 'I have said this before but you would not listen to me. Now several of my Ministers have informed me that they consider something should be done about you.'

'As I am English I cannot see anything I do should concern your Ministers or anyone else!' Roxana said defiantly.

'It concerns me,' the Governor replied slowly.

She loooked at him for a brief second, then looked away again. But before he spoke she knew that any suggestion he made would reflect his personal feelings for her which he could not disguise.

'What I think is undoubtedly reprehensible,' the Governor went on, 'is that you should live in what is in fact nothing but a native *balé.*'

'It was good enough for my uncle and my aunt when they arrived in this country.'

'Pieter Helderik was a Missionary,' the Governor answered in a contemptuous voice, 'but you, Roxana, are very different.'

'I am still a human being with my likes and dislikes. I am very happy here.'

'What I am prepared to offer you is a proper house,' the Governor said. 'It is empty at the moment because one of the officials who came here from Holland three years ago has had to return home.'

Roxana did not speak. She thought she knew the man to whom he referred.

'It is a very nice house,' the Governor went on, 'with every Western convenience which you do not have in a hovel like this.'

He paused and then added:

'It is also within the compound of Government House.'

There was a note in his voice that it was impossible to misunderstand.

Now, because she felt it was imperative to defy him, Roxana rose from the stool on which she had been sitting.

'Is that important?' she enquired, raising her chin as she faced the Governor.

'It is to me!' he replied.

'I am afraid I do not understand what Your Excellency is saying. I have already told you that I have not the time to work for you.'

'You are well aware of what I am trying to say,' he answered. 'I want you, Roxana, and, by God, I mean to have you!'

She did not flinch although she felt as

if she faced a wild beast.

'Your Excellency has a wife,' she said, and her voice was cold and unhurried. 'As you cannot offer me marriage, I cannot believe you would insult me by offering me anything else.'

'I will give you everything in the world you want,' the Governor said, 'not only a house, but money, jewels. You have only to ask.'

'Do you really believe that I would degrade myself by taking such a position in your or in any other man's life?'

'What is the alternative? To go on living like a peasant? To be ostracised by everyone out here who is civilised?'

'Are you suggesting they would accept me if I became your...mistress?'

'Then you would need no-one but me!' the Governor retorted.

'You must be mad to think that I could ever want you, or that you could ever mean anything in my life!' Roxana snapped. 'As I consider the suggestion you have made to me and the way you have spoken to me is a gross insult, I can only ask you to leave my house!'

The Governor made a sound that was almost like a growl.

'You should not treat me like this. If you will not do what I want of your own free will, then I will take other steps.'

'You are threatening me,' Roxana said, 'and I do not like it!'

'For God's sake why are we quarrelling?' the Governor asked savagely, 'I have no wish to threaten you. I am offering you everything that any other woman would find desirable.'

'You have offered me nothing!' Roxana replied. 'If you wish to do me a favour, leave me alone!'

'I have only to say the word and you will have to leave the island!'

'Then at least I shall not have to listen to your insults!'

She faced him defiantly and saw the anger growing in his look.

'You shall not speak to me like that!' he

replied, his voice rising.

He took a step towards her, and because Roxana thought he intended to take her in his arms she pointed the chisel she was holding in her hand towards him and held it level with her shoulder.

It was a thin, sharp-pointed tool which she used for intricate work and was almost as dangerous as a dagger.

The Governor appeared to realise this and although he came nearer he did not touch her.

'Would you really strike me?' he enquired after a moment.

'If you touch me I shall not hesitate to do so.'

'And you know what will happen to you?' he asked between gritted teeth.

'If I do not, I am sure you are longing to threaten me with some dire punishment.'

'Our prisons are not particularly comfortable places.'

'That I can well believe,' Roxana said scornfully.

'And when your prison sentence is over, you will be transported to your own country.'

For the first time since she had been defying the Governor, Roxana thought of Karel.

Too late she realised that she should have been conciliatory, playing for time.

Perhaps it was because she was so disappointed that he had called on her when she had been expecting the Count that she had not tried to appease him as she had done in the past, but said the first things which came into her head.

She knew he sensed that she was weakening.

Some of the anger went from his expression and he said in a different tone:

'Now you are coming to your senses! It is either prison, Roxana, or a very comfortable and pleasant existence in the house I have chosen for you.'

'That is impossible...completely impossible!' Roxana replied, feeling she must not let him think she was amenable at this point.

She lowered the hand that held the chisel.

'I will not strike at you,' she said, 'but I still have the freedom to refuse what you are offering me.'

'And you intend to go on living here, whatever I think about it?'

'Yes.'

'Then let me make it quite clear, I will not allow you to do so,' the Governor said. 'I want you, Roxana, and you have played with me for long enough! I will send servants and a carriage to collect you and your luggage to-morrow morning. If you refuse to come, I may resort to using force.'

Roxana lost her temper.

'How dare you order me about as if I were a slave!' she said stamping her foot. 'I am British, and if you attempt to behave in this manner towards me I will create an international incident which you will deeply regret.'

'To whom will you appeal?' the Governor asked, an unpleasant smile on his lips. 'The

British Consul in Djakarta? I can ensure that no letter of yours will ever reach him. Or would you prefer to appeal to the Governor of Malaya?'

He was deliberately baiting her, she thought, and yet like a cornered animal she was determined to go on fighting.

'Whatever you may say,' she replied, 'you need not waste your time sending a carriage for me or preparing a house in which I will not live. I would rather sleep on the hard ground than be beholden to you for anything!'

She almost spat the words at him and now the anger was back in the Governor's face, even though his eyes still glinted with the lust that was always there when he looked at her.

Unexpectedly he moved forward and, before she had time to raise her chisel again, his arms were around her, pinning hers to her sides.

She gave a little scream. At the same time she was afraid because of his strength, because of his over-powering proximity and her violent aversion which made her feel almost faint.

'Let me go!' she cried.

His arms only tightened and his lips sought hers.

She turned her head frantically from side to side, finding, because she was breathless with the horror of what was happening, that it was impossible to scream or do anything but try to fight, although she was helpless in his arms.

Then unexpectedly a voice said quietly and calmly behind them:

'So here you are, Your Excellency! I thought it was your carriage I saw outside.'

To Roxana it was as if an angel came down from the skies to deliver her and her heart leaped not only because she was saved but because the Count was there.

With a muttered oath the Governor took his arms from her and turned round.

The Count was standing below them in the court-yard and as the Governor faced him, a bellicose expression on his red face, he continued calmly in the courteous voice that he might have used in any Drawing-Room:

'The meeting you arranged for me finished earlier than I expected and I hope, as there are several questions I want to ask you, that we may travel back together.'

For the moment it seemed as if the Governor would make some rude and angry retort.

Then the Count's calm manner and the ease with which he stood looking up at him, made the discipline of years assert itself.

It was as if in a few fleeting seconds he remembered the Count's importance, his connection with the Queen Dowager, his own position as Governor.

There was the question too whether, as he had had his back to the court-yard, the Count had actually seen what was happening between him and Roxana.

With what was an obvious effort he said:

'As you suggest, we might as well return to Government House together.'

'That is excellent!' the Count exclaimed.

Then, as the Governor stepped from the raised floor of the Studio onto the court-yard, the Count acted as if he saw Roxana for the first time, and swept off his hat.

'Good-morning, Miss Barclay!' he exclaimed. 'I hope your carving is progressing, despite the heat.'

It was impossible for Roxana to reply.

She could only stand staring at him, her eyes, expressing both relief and love, seeming to fill her whole face.

'I shall look forward to seeing what progress you have made another time,' the Count went on. 'Now, you will understand that as I have business matters to discuss with His Excellency I must take him away.'

Just for a moment their eyes met and Roxana knew without words that he understood what she felt.

Then the Count turned and walked beside the Governor who was already crossing the court-yard.

'I was exceedingly impressed,' Roxana heard him say in his quiet cultured voice, 'by the progress you have already made, and I understand from what I heard this morning that...'

The two men passed through the gate-way and their voices died away in the distance.

It was then that Roxana sat down on her wooden stool as if her legs were going to give way under her.

He had saved her this time but she was aware that the Governor would not let it rest there.

She told herself that she had been foolish to defy him so openly; because her happiness, because her love for the Count had brought her a feeling of immunity she had perhaps been rash and over-courageous.

She walked into the house and realised with a sense of relief that Geertruida, intent on her cooking in the kitchen, was not aware of what had occurred.

She came into the *balé*, which served as a Sitting-Room, carrying a tray in her hands and saying:

'I hope you like what I've made you this

morning, Miss Roxana. It's a new way of cooking chicken which I found in one of the magazines we brought from home.'

'I am sure it is...delicious!' Roxana replied with an effort.

'It would be different if we had a nice, fat Dutch bird,' Geertruida went on. 'These skinny little creatures have no more flesh on them than sparrows.'

'It is plenty for me,' Roxana answered.

Geertruida put the tray down on one of the chests, laid the table with a white cloth and put a covered dish on it.

'Now eat it up while it's hot,' she said.

It was no use, Roxana had found out long ago, asking Geertruida to serve cold food in the heat of the day.

She believed in a good, hot meal for *het middadmaal* or luncheon, and Roxana knew her routine would be the same whether she was on the Equator or at the North Pole.

There was also, however, a big bowl of delicious fruit for her to choose from, and rather than disappoint Geertruida she put a small helping of the chicken on her plate.

Because of what she had been through she felt as if even a mouthful would choke her, but she managed to taste the chicken and say with a smile:

'It is delicious! You are clever, Geertruida, to find something new!'

'It's difficult enough in this place,' Geertruida replied, 'but your aunt always said I cooked with imagination, and that's what I try to do.'

She went away and quickly Roxana put most of what she had put on her plate back on the dish.

How could she eat, she asked herself, when she was confronted by such difficulties and by the thought that even though she had the Count's protection the Governor might still make himself unpleasant.

There was Karel, too, to think of, Karel to get away to safety, and for the first time she wondered if the Count would find the baby a nuisance.

Because even the thought of it frightened

Roxana, she decided she would go at once to the forest to see if Karel was all right.

She would hold him in her arms and perhaps in the mere closeness with him would find an answer to the questions which kept presenting themselves.

Without waiting for Geertruida to return she ran into the kitchen to find her.

'I am going to see Karel,' she said. 'I will not be away for long. If the Count comes to see me, please ask him to wait.'

She saw Geertruida's lips tighten and wondered why she disliked the Count. What he had done or not done in Holland was no concern of hers.

'She will change her mind when she knows him better,' Roxana told herself.

She set off towards the forest walking quickly, forgetting the heat and everything else because of her urgency to see Karel.

How much easier it would be, she thought, if only he could live with them, but it was far too dangerous to have him in her house when the Governor kept appearing unexpectedly.

What will the Count say, she wondered for the thousandth time as she reached the forest, when I ask him if we can take Karel with us when we leave the island?

Then almost as if she could actually hear her there was Geertruida's voice saying: 'Has he asked you to marry him?'

'How could he do anything else?' Roxana whispered fiercely. 'He is not like the Governor, and what we feel for each other is holy and sacred. Something which is part of the sacrament of marriage.'

She hurried up the twisting stone path which led to Ida Anak Temu's house.

As she expected, he was sitting outside on the raised platform surrounded by his craftsmen, all holding a piece of wood with their feet and working with the skill and speed that was characteristic of the Balinese carvers.

Ida Anak Temu had told Roxana when she first asked him to teach her that when a man carves, his soul goes into the wood so that no model is ever necessary.

To-day Ida Anak Temu was working on a mask.

He was a handsome old man with a *batik* cap set at a jaunty angle on his grey hair, and when Roxana appeared he looked up at her with inquisitive, humorous eyes.

His mouth, like that of all those who were working with him, was darkly stained with *betel* but there was no mistaking the kindness or the welcome in his smile.

Roxana greeted him, then, politely, because it is rude in Bali to hurry, she admired his mask which he was carving from wood—soft, light and strong—called *pule*.

She asked after the health of his wife and his small children and then, at last, the proprieties over, she was able to slip past the raised *balé* and into the tree-shaded compound behind where she knew Karel would be with the other children.

When she found him he was asleep, lying in the shade of a tree, looking more than ever in his nakedness like a small cupid.

She thought how beautiful he was and how sweet, and knelt down beside him looking at his fair lashes on his pink-and-white cheeks.

Then, as if she could not resist touching him, she lifted him gently into her arms and, sitting cross-legged as the Balinese women did, held him against her breast.

He stirred for a moment, put his thumb into his mouth and went to sleep again.

There was something in the warm, comforting contentment of the child which made Roxana want to cry.

She had to protect him. She had to look after him and if possible to take him to England.

She had already decided in her mind who would adopt him.

Her mother and her Aunt Agnes had a sister a great deal younger than they were who was unable to have a child.

She had had a fall out hunting soon after she was married and had nearly lost her life.

She had survived, but the doctors had told her that there was no hope of her ever having a family.

Fortunately she was married to an understanding man who loved her too much to let her injuries embitter their marriage.

Roxana was certain that her Aunt Nancy would be only too happy to bring up her nephew, and love him as his mother would have loved him.

But England was far away and they were here in an alien world except for the Balinese family who were sheltering Karel at the moment, and of course the Count.

'He will understand, I know he will understand,' Roxana told herself.

And yet, insidiously, doubts began to creep into her mind.

Supposing, while he was willing to marry her, although he had not said so, he would not be prepared to defy the laws of his own countrymen by smuggling an orphan out of Bali?

That question was frightening enough, but

despite every resolution to ignore it another one had to be faced: 'Suppose, like the Governor, he does not wish to marry you?'

After all, she had no reason to be sure that he thought her important enough.

Roxana had lived in Amsterdam long enough to know that the social protocol was almost sacred to those at Court and to the Dutch Burghers and their wives.

The Count was near the top of a pyramid that rose higher and higher until it reached the Queen.

Could she really expect that he, a relative of the Queen Dowager, an exceedingly wealthy man, and without doubt the most eligible bachelor in the country would be prepared, however perfect their love might be, to marry a girl of whom he knew nothing except that she was the Step-niece of a Missionary?

It was as if a cold hand clutched at Roxana's heart.

At the same time some pride in her blood made her vow to herself that she would not tell him who her parents were until he had accepted her for herself alone.

'How can I doubt him?' she asked.

And yet she knew that almost like a serpent in the Garden of Eden the doubt was already there.

Her back was against the tree and she leaned against it, settling Karel a little more comfortably and trying, for the moment, to let the peace of the forest bring her a solace she could not find in her thoughts.

The playing children had moved further away and some of the smaller ones, like Karel, had fallen asleep on the ground, their naked bodies making little patches of gold, their eyelashes very dark against their round faces.

There were no more beautiful children in the world than in Bali, but it was impossible not to see the difference between them and Karel, not only in their colour, but in the strength of their bodies.

Already Karel seemed broader-shouldered, thicker-set and Roxana knew that he would be like his father, a tall man and undoubtedly handsome.

It came to her mind, that was what her own children would look like, hers and the Count's, and she felt a warmth run through her like a streak of sunlight at the thought that one day she might be holding her own son and his in her arms.

She must have fallen asleep to dream not only of the Count but of his children, and when she opened her eyes it was as if, because he was there, she was still dreaming.

She looked up at him hazily, her mind for a moment asleep with her dreams.

Then as she saw the expression on his face she awoke almost with a bang to reality.

'Whose child is that?'

His voice was harsh and seemed to break not only the silence that surrounded them but to echo discordantly in the forest.

Roxana could only look up at him, finding it impossible to answer, feeling she must be still asleep, and this must be part of her dream.

But then the suspicion she saw in the Count's eyes and the harshness of his tone frightened her and in a sudden panic and without her conscious volition, she heard herself reply:

'He is mine! Mine!'

As she spoke she pulled Karel closer and he, too, awoke with a little murmur and struggled to free himself.

There was silence after she had spoken and she thought that the Count's face moved hazily in front of her. Then he asked, still in a voice that made her afraid:

'Who is his father?'

Again without thinking, driven only by a fear that she could not control Roxana answered:

'I...do not...know!'

She saw the expression of suspicion on the Count's face turn to one which she thought was disgust, then he turned and walked away and, because he moved swiftly, he left tiny clouds of dust with every footstep.

He was gone.

For a moment Roxana could not believe it had really happened that he had found her, he had asked her two questions and, because she dared not answer them truthfully, her world had fallen in pieces about her ears.

She felt that she was left in an impenetrable darkness which covered her like a shroud.

The pain of what had happened was so intolerable that for a long time she could only sit with her eyes closed knowing that Karel had crawled from her arms onto the ground and she was alone...utterly alone...

At last she knew she must do something.

She got to her feet as if she had suddenly become very old and youth had left her.

Slowly she walked to the *balé* in which Ida Anak Temu was still working.

'I want to speak to you in private.'

It was difficult to find the right words in Balinese but he understood and put down his knife. He rose and walked with her back into the tree-shaped compound.

'Help me...please help me,' Roxana pleaded.

He looked at her reflectively and while he did not speak she had the feeling he was sympathetic.

'I have to go away,' she said. 'If I stay, even though they do not find Karel, I may be put in prison or subjected to worse humiliations.'

Ida Anak Temu nodded his head as if he was aware without explanation that anything might be expected of their Dutch overlords.

'Where can I go? Tell me!' Roxana pleaded. 'Where can I go where the Governor will not find me.'

She hesitated, then she said:

'I must take Karel with me. His Excellency knows I am your pupil. If I disappear he may vent his anger on you.'

The old man looked at her and she knew without explanation that he understood what she was inferring where the Governor was concerned.

Very little could happen in Bali, which

even those who lived in isolation in the forests did not know.

The fact that the Governor was pursuing her was doubtless an open secret amongst them.

'Where can I go?' Roxana asked frantically.

Ida Anak Temu thought for a moment, then he spoke one word:

'Badung!'

Roxana stared.

'South Bali? But how can I get there?'

She thought, even as she asked the question, that the Dutch would try to prevent those who lived in the North from crossing to the independent South over which they had no authority.

'There is a way,' Ida Anak Temu replied.

Roxana looked at him eagerly.

'You will show me? You will tell me how I can find it?'

The old man was silent for a moment, concentrating in the same way that he concentrated his soul on his work. Then he said:

'Njoman will take you.'

Njoman, Roxana knew, was one of his sons, a strong young man who was mainly concerned with cutting down and bringing wood for his father, his craftsman brothers and their apprentices.

'That is very kind of you,' Roxana said. 'When can we go?'

'At day-light.'

'We will be ready. I will take Karel back with me now.'

Again Ida Anak Temu nodded and Roxana looked away from him to where Karel was crawling towards another child of about the same age who was playing happily with some leaves and a few coloured pieces of wood.

'How can I...thank you for your...kindness?' she asked in a low voice.

Ida Anak Temu smiled, and even with his *betel*-stained lips there was something very warming about it.

'You have eyes in your soul,' he said. 'Such pupils are rare!'

It was a very great compliment spoken in the Balinese language and Roxana reached out and took his gnarled old hand in hers.

'I shall thank you until my dying day,' she said. 'When I have gone, will you look after my carvings?'

He nodded and she added:

'Anything that must be left behind, if it is of any use, is yours. I am sure we can only take a very little of what we own with us.'

For the first time she wondered if they must travel on foot, and as if he realised what she was thinking of Ida Anak Temu said:

'Njoman will bring a *gharry* but be ready by the first light.'

'Tell him we will be waiting,' Roxana said.

She picked up Karel as she spoke and because he was happy at his game, he made a little cry of protest.

As she held him Ida Anak Temu cried out:

'Soka!' and his eldest daughter came from a *balé* hidden amongst the trees.

He gave her quick instructions and she returned with a sarong that she wrapped around Karel, covering him completely so that only his small face could be seen.

Roxana thanked her because she knew it was Soka who had looked after Karel with her own children.

She wished she had something to give her as a present, then she remembered she was wearing a small pearl brooch at the neck of her gown.

It was not a valuable piece of jewellery, but to Soka, because it was different from anything she had ever owned before, it might have been a gem from the golden crown of the Priest in the Temple.

She thanked Roxana so effusively that she was embarrassed and hurried away because she knew there would be a great deal to do when she arrived home.

She thought she would return, as she had come, alone, but Ida Anak Temu insisted on sending one of his granddaughters with her.

Roxana knew this was because if anything happened on the way, if anyone should question her because she carried Karel in her arms, the child would return and tell her grandfather what had happened.

It was not only, she knew, a protection for her own safety, but also for Njoman, in case when he arrived with the *gharry* at the break of light he was accused of smuggling someone out of the North.

It was over two months since Roxana had taken Karel, on his father's death to hide in the forest.

He had grown much heavier in the ensuing time and before they reached her house her arms were aching.

She looked tentatively into the court-yard before she entered it just in case either the Governor or the Count was waiting for her, but she guessed it was unlikely as there was no carriage or horse outside.

As Geertruida came hurrying from the kitchen at her approach, there was astonishment on her face when she saw what Roxana carried in her arms. However, she walked past the old maid only saying:

'Give the little girl some eggs and fruit and when she has gone shut the gate!'

'Shut the gate?' Geertruida exclaimed in surprise.

But she knew the order concerned Karel and she did as Roxana told her and came a few minutes later into the Sitting-*balé* looking anxious.

'What's happened? Is Karel ill? Why have you brought him home?'

'We are leaving to-morrow, at break of day.'

'Where are we going?'

'To Badung in the South.'

Geertruida looked astonished and Roxana explained:

'The Count followed me into the forest. Did you tell him where I was going?'

'No, of course not!' Geertruida said angrily. 'Do you think I'd do anything so foolish?'

'Then how did he know where to come?'

Geertruida thought for a moment.

'I thought I heard the sound of a horse's

hoofs in the court-yard soon after you left. It took me a few minutes to put down what I was doing and when I looked there was no-one there.'

'The Count must have come to see me,' Roxana said, almost as if she spoke to herself, 'and I suppose if he asked the children who are usually playing outside in the road they would have told him where I had gone.'

'That's more than likely!' Geertruida snapped. 'It's impossible to keep anything to oneself in Bali!'

Roxana was sure that was what had happened and then she remembered that she had let Ida Anak Temu's name slip when she had been talking to the Count and he would guess that was where he would find her.

Anyone he met in the forest would direct him willingly to the Master-craftsman.

Everyone in this part of Bali was proud of his achievements and filled with admiration for his carvings.

'Why was I such a fool as to go there this

afternoon, of all days?' Roxana asked herself.

Then she knew that there was no time for regrets of recriminations.

She had lost the Count. She had lost the love he had brought her.

There was only one thing which must concern her at the moment and that was to get Karel to safety.

At the same time her body, her heart, her mind and her soul cried out because she had lost what had proved to be a brief dream.

But the memory of it would remain with her, she knew in the long, lonely years ahead.

CHAPTER SIX

As the Count rode through the forest he was seething with rage. In fact he was so angry that his whole body was shaking with fury.

He had believed in Roxana, in her perfection and her purity, and had lain awake almost all night thinking of her.

He had told himself he had found somebody so unique, so unusual, that she was like a gift from the Gods.

When he had walked into the court-yard and seen that something was occurring between her and the Governor, his first impulse was to tell His Excellency what he thought of him and even knock him down.

Then the years of diplomatic training, of practising self control which had become instinctive, made him realise that, for Roxana's sake, the last thing he must do was to cause a scene.

Because they were at the end of the Studio and he could not see very clearly, he was not, in fact, entirely sure of what was happening or if, as he suspected, the Governor was trying to kiss Roxana.

He had dealt with the situation in what he thought was a tactful manner and made it impossible for His Excellency to take offence.

He was aware that the elder man was annoyed from the way in which he flung himself down in his carriage and, for a short while after the horses drove off, made no attempt at conversation.

Then, as if he decided to make certain the situation did not react unfavourably against him he said:

'I am sure you will be interested to hear, Count, that I have solved the problem of Miss Barclay.'

'How have you done that?'

'I have persuaded her to leave that village

217

shack in which she is at present living and move into an excellent house that has fortunately become available.'

'And she has agreed to that?' the Count asked.

'She is, of course, delighted,' the Governor replied, 'and the fact that she will be in the compound of Government House will put paid to many of the unpleasant rumours that have been circulating about her.'

The Count did not reply to this and after he had waited for his comments the Governor went on:

'Of course, you and I, as men of the world, are well aware that Miss Barclay's appearance is bound to cause unfavourable comment amongst the ladies.'

He gave a short laugh. Then he said:

'Although, unfortunately, I must admit that there are some reasons for their antagonism.'

'What do you mean by that?' the Count enquired, deliberately making his voice expressionless.

'Well, naturally there is talk of a number of lovers, for one thing,' the Governor said, 'all of them, needless to say, undesirable, and my wife told me before she left there was even a rumour that Miss Barclay had a child!'

It was with difficulty that the Count resisted an impulse to strike him in the face.

How dare anyone say such things about Roxana?

He was quite prepared to believe it was just jealousy, and yet he was astute enough to understand that in a small community jealousy could smoulder beneath the surface for a long time before it burst into a dangerous and all-consuming flame.

'I am sure that is untrue, at any rate,' he remarked.

The Governor shrugged his shoulders.

'One never knows with the English,' he said. 'They appear to be icebergs, then, often one is pleasantly surprised.'

He spoke as if he was reminiscing about something he had enjoyed and again the

Count longed to strike him, but knew that if he did so he would immediately have to leave Bali.

He decided that he would get in touch with Roxana and warn her that she must be careful and also they must make plans for their future.

The Count had not really decided if he would ask Roxana to marry him.

For years he had been pursued by people wanting to pressurise him into marriage from all sides and he had grown wary and extremely careful of himself.

It was not only his mother who begged him with tears in her eyes to settle down or his other relations who continually pointed out to him that he was head of a large and important family, and the sooner he added to their number the better.

There was also the Queen Dowager.

'You must marry, Viktor,' she had said several times before the unfortunate incident of Luise van Heydberg. 'You know as well as I do that you are a disturbing influence at Court. You are far too handsome and far too attractive. A wife is what you need.'

'And you think she will control me?' the Count asked with a smile.

'It would be a brave woman who attempted to do that,' the Queen Dowager replied, 'but at least you would be able to offer a more respectable front to the world than you do at the moment.'

The Count laughed but it merely strengthened his resolve that nobody should force him into marriage, nor would he ask any woman to be his wife until he was certain she was exactly the person he required.

He was not quite certain what that would be. In the world in which he lived marriage was one thing—love another.

As the Countess van Haan, his wife, would have a position at court that was unassailable, and also, from a woman's point of view, extremely enjoyable.

There were, of course, certain hereditary Royal duties she would be expected to execute.

At the same time every door in Holland would be open to her and she would automatically, next to the Queen and the Queen Dowager, have the best place at every Theatre, every Opera, every race-meeting, every entertainment in which she might be interested.

She would also have the privilege, which the Count always found pleasant, of offering hospitality to every distinguished person who visited the country.

What was more, she would be welcomed in the most exclusive circles in Paris and in England and any other country in Europe she might care to visit.

At the same time the Count had no intention of saddling himself with a wife whose only assets were her good breeding and her ability to play hostess for him in a manner that would gain the admiration of his friends.

The Count had often been spoken of as a perfect host and he therefore told himself that that part of his wife's duty would not be arduous.

What he had to consider was whether he would find her interesting and attractive when they were alone.

He had admitted to himself last night that he was in love, in a way that intrigued and at the same time mystified him.

What was it that was different about Roxana? he questioned, and knew the answer was that she evoked in him emotions that he had never known before.

Because he had grown cynical where women were concerned, he asked himself if the magic he had felt when he kissed her under the frangipani tree was not in fact due to the strange feelings he had felt during the performance of the *Ketjak*.

He knew that what he had felt then had also been due to Roxana.

It was because she was with him, because they were feeling and understanding the same things, because the touch of her hand had been more exciting and more sensational than anything he had ever known before.

'I love her!' the Count admitted.

He cursed the fact that the Governor had arranged a round of duties for him and a luncheon with a number of men that on other occasions he might have found interesting.

He hurried away from the luncheon thinking that it was an opportunity to see Roxana alone before he was expected back at Government House.

When he saw the Governor's carriage outside the door of the compound it had annoyed him because he suspected that he had deliberately called at a time when visitors were not usually expected.

But now driving back towards Government House the Count decided that if the Governor was prepared to cheat then he would do the same thing.

'I have quite a lot of reports to write this afternoon, Your Excellency,' he said, 'so I hope you will excuse me until perhaps five o'clock.'

'That will suit me,' the Governor replied, 'and there will be several people coming in later to meet you.'

As he spoke, they entered the elaborate gates that led into the huge compound in which Government House was situated.

The usual mud wall encircled it and there were sentries at the gate who presented arms as they passed.

They drove up a smooth drive which was very different from many of the other roads on which they travelled.

Then when Government House was in sight the Governor pointed to where, a little to the left of it, there was a small house encircled with trees.

'That will be Miss Barclay's house,' he said.

There was a note of satisfaction in his voice which the Count disliked.

It was, however, undoubtedly a very attractive house with a wide verandah over which there was growing a profusion of bougainvillea.

The Count did not miss the fact that it was conveniently close to the Governor, and there was also a thick foilage of trees and shrubs between the two houses which he was sure would prove a useful conceal-ment.

His lips tightened and he told himself forcefully that he must take Roxana away. But where to? And would she be prepared to travel with him even if it was possible to do so?

'I have to think this out sensibly,' the Count told himself.

He found himself wishing that he had met Roxana in Holland or in England. He wanted to see her in his own environment and hers before he made any important de-cision about her.

He would like her to meet his mother and to be introduced to her relations.

He found himself thinking of the straw-covered *balés* which were her home at the moment and comparing them with his large and impressive house in Amsterdam, his home in the country which had belonged to his ancestors, his large and very luxurious apartment in Paris.

They were all ready for him to use at a moment's notice and he also possessed a Hunting Lodge in Bavaria where he had given many enjoyable parties.

How could he know what Roxana would be like in these places?

And how could he be sure that what he felt for her was not just an infatuation that like a tropical flower would not survive in a colder and more austere climate?

He had, therefore, every intention of putting his feelings to the test by seeing her as soon as possible.

When he left the Governor walked away to his own rooms, which were in a different part of the building, he told a servant to have a horse brought to a side door.

The Count had no compunction about spending his time, when he considered himself to be off duty, as he pleased.

As soon as the horse arrived he mounted and rode down a different path from the one by which he had approached the house with the Governor.

He also moved among the trees which made it very unlikely that anyone would notice his departure.

He arrived at Roxana's house and one glance at the Studio told him that she was not working.

Then as he swung himself from the saddle the boy who held his horse on other occasions came from a different *balé* to say:

'Missie out!'

He spoke in Dutch and the Count asked.

'Where has she gone?'

For a moment the boy looked puzzled. Then with a smile because he understood he pointed with his finger to the east.

The Count knew it was in the direction of the forest and guessed that Roxana had gone to visit her teacher.

Without wasting any more time he remounted and rode towards the forest thinking it would be interesting to meet Ida Anak Temu, whose name he remembered, and see how his work compared with that of his pupil.

It was not difficult to find people who could direct him to Ida Anak Temu's house, but he found it was impossible to ride all the way.

Fortunately he found a boy whom he was able to put in charge of his horse and then he started to climb up the rocky path which Roxana had traversed so often.

He must have nearly reached Ida Anak Temu's *balé* when he heard the voices of children and took what he realised afterwards was the wrong fork of the path.

To find the Master-craftsman he should have gone straight on, but instead he went towards the children's voices and soon found them tumbling about in the forest.

They were laughing happily with childish joy and their nakedness made them, as Roxana had thought, look like small cupids.

There were several older children with them wearing sarongs but they paid no attention to him and he walked on a little further expecting to find Ida Anak Temu.

It was then he saw Roxana asleep beneath

a tree, and she had, incredibly, a baby in her arms that was white-skinned and fair-haired.

Everything that the Governor had said came back to him with a shock that seemed to vibrate through him.

So it was true! She had a child!

She had not been pure and innocent as he had thought her to be when he had drawn her into his arms and believed, incredible though it seemed, that he was the first man who had ever kissed her.

There was something so inexperienced, and yet so wonderful, in the surrender of her lips that it had never for one moment struck him there could have been a man in her life before.

Yet now she was holding the sleeping child protectively and the mere fact that his head was against her breast made the Count think they were linked together by blood.

He stood staring at her, at the darkness of her eye-lashes against her cheeks, the russet lights in her hair, her thin, sensitive fingers which held the child.

Then she had opened her eyes...

★ ★ ★ ★

As he rode away the Count cursed himself for being a fool, for being deceived as he told himself he had never been deceived before.

Roxana's words were in his mind and seemed to echo in his ears, but worst of all, and most humiliating was that she had admitted she did not know who the child's father was.

The Governor had spoken of her lovers. One of them must have been fair-haired and in every probability Dutch.

The Count told himself he hated her.

By her perfidy she had destroyed something within him that had been so beautiful and so glorious that he could hardly believe he had lost it and it was something he would never find again.

'I hate her!' he tried to say over and over again, and rode on until he found the tree-bordered road which led towards

Government House.

But he had only to think of the spiritual expression on her face, of the things they had discussed together, the fire that had burnt in them both when he touched her hand, to know it was not hatred he felt but something very different.

At Government House he had sent his Valet for brandy and drank it in a manner which made the man look at him in surprise.

He had never known his master to be anything but abstemious; in fact, he could never recall an occasion when he had drunk so early in the afternoon.

Somehow, the Count could never afterwards remember exactly what had happened.

He had made himself talk to the people who had been invited to meet him. He endured another long dinner with the same guests whom he had met a dozen times before and managed to appear as if he was enjoying himself and even to laugh at the

Governor's jokes.

When at last he had been able to go to his own room and be alone, he resisted an impulse to ride in the darkness to Roxana's house and see if after all he had been mistaken.

Then violently he thought that she would not deceive him again and that as far as he was concerned everything that had existed between them was over.

He slept very little in the morning, owing to the amount of brandy he had drunk and a troubled mind, he felt ill and extremely disagreeable.

'You can start packing,' he said to his Valet when he was dressed. 'The sooner we leave this place the better!'

'Where shall we be going, *Mijnheer*?' the man enquired.

'Singapore—India—what does it matter?' the Count enquired irritably. 'Just do as you are told and pack my things!'

He walked out of the room and the Valet shook his head.

His master never behaved like this and he knew that something was very wrong.

The Count walked towards the Breakfast-Room.

He usually ate alone, but this morning he could not bear his own company. Besides, he wished to inform the Governor that he was leaving.

Breakfast was served not in the room itself but outside on the wide verandah.

It was cool and pleasant at this early hour.

As the Count went in through the door he saw the Governor sitting with his back to him on the verandah and beside him, standing stiffly in his uniform, was the Officer in Charge of the sentries.

'Take a carriage, no, two carriages. You will want one for the luggage and Miss Barclay's maid,' the Governor was saying.

Almost instinctively the Count stood still.

'Stand no nonsense,' the Governor went on. 'If she will not come willingly use force, discreetly, of course, but do not listen to any protests she might make.

Do you understand?'

'Yes, Your Excellency, I understand,' the Officer said.

He spoke in a doubtful voice as if he found it a difficult assignment.

'Later, perhaps this afternoon,' the Governor continued, 'you can go back for the rest of her belongings, her wood-carving for instance and any furniture which she may wish to bring to the house.'

'Very good, Your Excellency!'

'One more thing...' the Governor went on, but the Count did not hear what he was about to say.

He turned and moved quietly back the way he had come.

The use of the word "force" was enough to tell him what the Governor was about and he knew whatever he might feel about her, in whatever way she had deceived him, he could not let this happen to Roxana.

He went to his own room and found his servant already packing.

'Get my horse quickly!' the Count snapped.

The man hurried to do his bidding.

The Count was waiting impatiently at the side door when the groom came from the stables, leading the horse he had ridden the day before.

As he rode off, taking the route he had used the previous afternoon, the Count told himself he would have to hurry.

He had not formed any particular plan in his mind about what he would do or how he could help Roxana.

He only knew that the thought of the Governor's power over her revolted him and every nerve in his body told him that he would not let her be imprisoned in a house conveniently within a few minutes' walk of the Governor's own apartments.

Whatever she might have been to other men, the Count was well aware, as was very understandable, that she was revolted by the Governor and his feelings for her.

He rode with all possible speed towards

the small village and through it to where Roxana's house was situated.

It was hot and his horse was sweating when finally he arrived.

He rode into the court-yard, then stared in astonishment to see a cart outside Roxana's Studio drawn by two bullocks. Two men were engaged in lifting her carving into the cart.

He dismounted and went towards them.

'What is happening?' he asked sharply.

They put the torso of the man carefully down before they looked up at him respectfully with no understanding in their expressions.

'Where is Miss Barclay?' the Count enquired knowing they had not understood.

The elder of the two men was smiling.

'Miss Barclay—gone!' he said.

'Where has she gone?'

The man shook his head, then after some seconds, as if he sought for the word with his very limited vocabulary, he said in Dutch:

'A-way—gone a-way!'

The Count stared at him, then leaving his horse unattended he walked towards the *balé* which Roxana used as a Sitting-Room.

He knew at once there was no-one there and he passed through it to find as he had expected that it was connected with another *balé* and which he saw must have been her Bed-room.

But it was empty, a cupboard door stood open and that was empty too.

He stared about him, then deliberately searched the rest of the building.

There was no-one anywhere and he found where Geertruida must have slept but the room contained no clothes.

He walked back into the court-yard and by now the bullock-cart was almost full of Roxana's carvings.

The Count walked onto the raised floor and went towards the table where she had kept the little carvings that she had told him she gave as presents.

He was thinking of the goddess fashioned

in sandalwood that she had said would protect him and he looked down at the delicate little hand she had carved with its curved fingers.

He picked it up and knew he must keep it and thought with a sudden panic that perhaps it would be all of her that he would ever possess.

Holding the hand he stepped back into the court-yard and took hold of the bridle of his horse.

It was no use talking to the two men in charge of the bullock-cart, because he knew he could not make them understand.

He walked through the gate-way, then saw with a leap of his heart Ponok coming towards him from the village.

He realised when Ponok had taken them to see the *Ketjak* that he was an intelligent man and he thought that perhaps he could make him understand what he wanted to know.

'Where is Miss Barclay, Ponok?' he enquired abruptly.

Ponok bowed to him politely.

'Gone!' he said even as the boys with the bullock-cart had said.

'Where? And why so quickly?'

He saw that Ponok did not understand.

He looked at the man and as if he showed how desperately he wanted an answer to his question Ponok held up his hand.

'Wait here!' he said.

He spoke in Balinese, but his gesture made the Count aware of what he was saying.

He nodded and Ponok ran back into the village.

Some minutes elapsed and the Count stood under the shade of the trees holding the bridle of his horse and trying frantically to think what had happened.

He was certain that he and the Governor between them had driven Roxana away.

But where had she gone? Unless, as he half-suspected, she was with Ida Anak Temu.

He decided that as soon as Ponok return-ed, unless he had anything definite to tell him, he would go to the forest and find the wood-carver and ask him what he knew.

Then when he was beginning to think that the man had forgotten about him he saw Ponok returning and with him an elderly man who had a stiff leg and could not walk very quickly.

The Count led his horse towards them and when they met the elderly man said in quite passable Dutch:

'*Guten morgan, Mijnheer.* I am Kantor, the Overseer of the village.'

The Count heaved a sigh of relief.

He knew that the Dutch had appointed Overseers in the villages whom they paid and naturally they chose men who could speak their language.

'I am the Count van Haan,' he said. 'I am a guest of His Excellency the Governor. I had arranged to see Miss Roxana Barclay this morning, but I understand she has left.'

The Overseer had a long conversation with Ponok which seemed to the Count to go on for an infuriatingly long time. Then at last the Overseer said:

'Ponok tells me, *Mijnheer*, that he does not wish to make any trouble for Miss Barclay, but she told him you were her friend so we feel that we can trust you.'

'I promise you,' the Count said solemnly, 'that I would do nothing to hurt or harm Miss Barclay in any way.'

The Overseer translated this to Ponok, who burst into a long speech which was punctuated only by a continuous nodding of the Overseer's head to show he understood.

When at last Ponok came to the end of what he was saying the Count, as if he could contain himself no longer, asked:

'Where is she? What has happened to her?'

'Ponok say,' the Overseer replied, 'that Miss Barclay and older lady leave at daybreak in *gharry*. He see go but think they want no good-byes.'

'Where did they go?' the Count asked.

The Overseer glanced at Ponok and the Count noticed an almost imperceptible movement which said "no".

'Listen,' he said insistently, 'I have to learn what has happened to Miss Barclay because I have something of the greatest importance to tell her.'

The Overseer translated this, but though the Count watched Ponok's face he felt the man was not impressed.

'Plead with him,' he said to the Overseer. 'Make him understand that I will pay him anything he asks, but it is for Miss Barclay's sake that I must know where she has gone.'

Again the Overseer translated and again the Count thought despairingly there was no response from Ponok.

Then he said:

'The Governor is sending soldiers. They may be here at any minute to convey Miss Barclay to Government House.'

He saw the startled expression in the Overseer's eyes. Then with a very different note in his voice from the way he had spoken before he told Ponok what the Count had said.

The two men exchanged words with a swiftness and a fluency that was almost bewildering, then the Overseer said:

'Ponok believe you good friend to Miss Barclay, but he say not worry. She safe.'

'How can you know that?'

'What is the time, *Mijnheer?*'

The Count could not understand what that had to do with the question, but because he was determined to be conciliatory and some-how extract the information he wanted from the two men he looked at his watch.

'It is just after nine o'clock,' he said.

Both men stared at his watch, then Ponok said a few words to the Overseer, and he must have told him he could now speak, for the man said:

'Ponok say Miss Barclay take her clothes with her in *gharry*'

'What does that mean?' the Count asked.

'They go long way,' the Overseer replied.

'But where? Where have they gone?'

'Ponok not sure, but think Miss Barclay go by secret road that lead to mountains.'

'To the mountains?' the Count repeated in bewilderment. 'But where in the mountains?'

The Overseer took a step nearer to him, then in a voice so low he could hardly hear it he said:

'The South where no Dutch!'

★ ★ ★ ★

The route they were taking was very beautiful and at any other time Roxana would have been thrilled and interested to be moving higher and higher up the stony, winding road which climbed up from the rice fields.

They passed a few women at the beginning of the ascent walking in single file, proudly balancing heavy baskets on their heads.

But after that there was only the wild beauty of the mountains towering above them, which Roxana knew Njoman thought were filled with gods, strange spirits and vindictive demons who might attack them at any moment.

Every village through which they passed looked like a miniature fortress, each one surrounded by a wall five feet high and crowned with thatch.

This was erected as a protection against evil spirits which were known to crawl on the ground.

The first night they stayed in a village with a relative of Ida Anak Temu's who welcomed them profusely but with an undeniable curiosity, as if they had stepped down from the mountains.

The entrance to the village was exceedingly narrow, allowing enough passage for only one person at a time.

The *gharry* had to be left outside, but the horse which had drawn it came in with them.

Inside the gate stood a further brick screen intended to catch and hold any malevolent genie who might have succeeded in stepping over the threshold.

To make quite certain that the villagers

were protected, out of the sea of greenery there projected numerous thin poles of bamboo canes from which dangled bunches of lucky charms of all shapes and sizes.

They travelled a long way the first day so as to be well clear of any Dutchmen who might have asked where they were going and turn them back.

Roxana was aware that Njoman was nervous and continually urged on his horse which was a smaller animal than those in any other part of the world.

It was Geertruida who had solved the problem of what they should take with them.

Ignoring all the innumerable leather trunks which had carried their clothes from England she had instead wrapped Roxana's gowns and her own in clean linen sheets.

These filled the back of the *gharry* but even so Roxana felt ashamed that they should impose such a heavy load on such a small animal.

But the horse was certainly stronger than

it appeared, and incredibly quickly they had climbed from the flat ground up the side of the mountain and from a hot, moist heat into what had first seemed a welcome cold temperature.

But that night they wrapped themselves in all the warm clothes they possessed and as Roxana and Geertruida lay side by side on a straw mattress they cuddled Karel between them.

The next day, having thanked their hosts and left them with a sum of money which caused them incredulous delight, they set off at day-break.

It was fortunate that Roxana had plenty of money.

When they had first come to Bali her uncle had decided that he would place everything he had brought with him in safe-keeping.

But this he had found meant handing it over to the Dutch authorities and he had the feeling that they might question or restrict what he spent.

He soon learnt that the Balinese either

kept their money in the thatch of their roofs or they merely dug a hole in the ground and buried it.

There were practically no thieves in the country and Roxana learned later that it was not until the Dutch arrived that there was crime of any sort in this island Paradise.

The doors in the village in which they lived were furnished with neither locks nor bolts.

Jails which were built by the Dutch were very small and serious criminals had to be sent to a penitentiary in Java.

Roxana had therefore quickly dug up the floor of one of the *balés* for the money which her uncle had brought with him.

She herself had a considerable sum hidden in the thatch of her Bed-room and the rest was left carelessly in a drawer where it had not been touched.

'We have enough to last us for months, even years if necessary,' she told Geertruida.

'There's no need, all the same, to be extravagant, Miss Roxana,' Geertruida replied automatically.

It meant that on the journey they could be generous to those who were not only giving them hospitality but also protecting them.

The second day Roxana saw for the first time in the distance the impressive outline of the volcano Batur, which, she was told, stood nine thousand feet high.

She wondered if she would ever have the chance to see it and perhaps to visit the famous Temple which she had heard nestled at the foot of it.

But at the moment she was too concerned with getting on and knowing that they were safe in Badung.

The island was only fifty miles in width from the North Coast to the South but they could not travel many miles a day as some of the route was so rough that their horse could only move at a walking pace.

It was also quite obvious by the third day that if they were tired of travelling the horse was too.

Fortunately there was always a village in which Ida Anak Temu's name was known. Sometimes they stayed with his relatives, sometimes merely with admiring fans who were honoured that any pupil of his should grace their *balé*.

With the exception of the manner in which the inhabitants chewed *betal* and spat it out, everything was spotlessly clean.

Even so Geertruida insisted on spreading one of their own sheets on the native bed which she and Roxana usually had to share.

But they were so tired that Roxana often thought that if they had to lie on the bare floor she would still have slept peacefully.

Because of her feeling of unhappiness about the Count, she had expected to lie awake thinking of him, longing for him and feeling the desperate desolation which had swept over her when he had walked away and left her in the forest.

But it was almost as if the fatigue of the journey, the long hours that she had to nurse Karel and the strain of escaping had for the moment numbed her emotions.

Sometimes when she thought of the Count she felt for a brief second as if there was a dagger piercing her breast, so sharp, so agonising that she must scream with the pain of it.

Then Karel would need attention or Geertruida would talk in her sane, sensible manner, and Roxana would find the ordinary, commonplace things kept her mind from the agony of her soul.

The third day they left the cold behind and began descending into the moist, warm atmosphere and brilliant sunshine.

Rice fields appeared, plants and shrubs were bright with blossom, and the peasants they passed seemed to move more slowly with graceful languor which proclaimed that any effort was fatiguing.

Another night in a rather larger village, then in the distance there was the blue of the sea and the horse seemed to quicken its pace because their destination was in sight.

Roxana had learned from Njoman that

they were to go on to a large village near the sea. This was where Ida Anak Temu's most brilliant pupil lived, who already had gained a great reputation as a carver.

When they found Gueda Tano, he was obviously excited to meet Roxana and to see Njoman again. From the moment they stepped into his compound he wanted Roxana to admire his work.

In his home there were a dozen *balés* and more shrines than Roxana had ever seen before.

He seemed to be very prosperous and Njoman told her that he expected when Ida Anak Temu died that he would be the most famous carver in the whole of Bali.

Roxana was extremely impressed with his work, although she thought, or perhaps she was prejudiced, that it was not quite as good as his teacher's.

Nevertheless it was impossible to acknowledge that some of his carvings were magnificent, and she had a sudden longing to show them to the Count and hear his opinion.

When all the courtesies had been completed and refreshments had been served to them by Gueda Tano, Roxana asked if he could advise her of a house she could buy or rent.

He smiled with delight and assured her that such a request was easy. If she could pay there were plenty of *balés* that were too expensive for the ordinary villagers.

She assured him that she was prepared to pay anything that was reasonable, and as if he had been almost leading up to this moment Gueda Tano told her that there was a house in a compound adjoining his own.

It had previously been occupied by his elder son, but he and his family had gone to Singapore.

Roxana looked surprised and he explained:

'My son very clever. He painter, wish sell his paintings. There no sale in Bali—walls not strong enough hold painting in frames.'

This was true enough and they all laughed. A framed picture could not hang on the bamboo screens which were usually taken up or lowered in accordance with changes of sun or climate.

He brought a picture to show Roxana an example of the work his son was doing, and she saw at once that it was not only beautiful but also unusual. She was quite certain that he would find a ready market amongst the British in Singapore.

It was also a relief to find that she had not to go any further.

The house would suit them admirably and Gueda Tano promised he would lend them anything they wanted until they had time to buy new for themselves.

'What I want,' Geertruida said when they were out of hearing of their chattering host, 'is a kitchen where I can cook a decent meal!'

Roxana had been too unhappy on the journey to worry what she ate, but Geertruida found the invariable rice, the sea-turtle and the coconut milk not only monotonous but unpalatable.

Roxana knew that had their hosts been aware of their coming they would have killed a sucking-pig, but that took time.

Usually, as they arrived when darkness was beginning to fall, all they wanted was something light to eat and a chance to put their heads down.

Karel slept peacefully on the journey, the swing of the *gharry* seemed to rock him to sleep and while he was with Ida Anak Temu he had learnt to enjoy coconut milk.

That was readily available and was always fresh.

While Geertruida complained that it was not enough for a growing child, there was obviously nothing wrong with a baby who smiled, slept and awoke to smile again.

Only when they had moved into the house next door to Gueda Tano and Njoman had departed back to the North with a present that made him speechless with surprise, and Geertruida had enough cooking utensils to make her happy, did Roxana find time to think about herself.

Then the agony within her breast was no longer numb.

She missed the Count with an intensity that made her feel that she was in an impenetrable darkness and alone as she had never been alone before in her whole life.

She had always thought that love would be quiet and peaceful; a warm cosy happiness.

But ever since she had known the Count, love was something very different; magical, mystical, ecstatic, a lifting of her whole being towards the heights she had never dreamt existed.

Now she had dropped into the depths of misery and despair and she felt as if every inch of her body was cut and wounded by a thousand knives.

'I love him! I love him!' she whispered and wondered why his love had not been big enough to forgive or even understand.

Geertruida had been right. She had to make sure that he was trustworthy before she revealed the secret of Karel.

Fortunately for the child's sake she had not told him the truth.

She was convinced now that the Count would have denounced them all to the Dutch authorities and Karel would have been taken from them.

Doubtless he would have been conveyed to an Orphanage in Java from which it would have been impossible to rescue him.

She tried to tell herself that the fact that Karel was now safe should be a satisfaction in itself and she should ask nothing more of the gods.

But that did not assuage the ache within her, the void that seemed to fill her body and the tears which made her sob when she was alone until she was exhausted.

How was it possible that she had found Paradise for one ecstatic moment under the frangipani tree to lose it in the forest the very next day?

She had only to shut her eyes to see the suspicion in the Count's face as he looked at her, to hear the harshness of his questions, to see his expression of anger and disgust as he turned to walk away.

She told herself that the only thing that mattered now was not the past but the future.

Somehow she must leave Bali and get Karel back to England.

It would certainly not be as difficult as it had seemed when they were in the North of the island, but she learnt the first day they were in Badung that the ships which called at the port were mostly Dutch.

Occasionally, she learned, there were English steamers, but they were usually not passenger ships.

She would just have to wait and hope that by some lucky chance a cargo vessel would come into port which could be persuaded to take them to Singapore, or there might be a trader of another nationality.

Her hopes were not particularly optimistic, and Roxana told herself she must just be resigned to staying where they were until good fortune smiled on her again.

Because it was impossible to sit about doing nothing and Geertruida looked after

Karel so well that he needed little attention from her, Roxana brought the wood she wanted from the men who supplied Gueda Tano and started work.

She looked at various pieces of wood to find that her soul saw only one thing inside them—the Count's face.

She told herself she was being ridiculous but it was inescapable.

She tried smaller pieces of wood and saw his hand.

Finally she capitulated and started to carve him, finding a pleasure that was almost wholly pain in chiselling out his fine features, the noble height of his forehead, the balanced curve of his head.

'Can't you find anyone else to do?' Geertruida asked sharply.

Roxana did not answer and she said:

'You may think you are unhappy now, but one day you will realise you have had a lucky escape.'

'What have you got against the Count?' Roxana asked.

She found, even though Geertruida condemned him, it was somehow a relief to talk about it because there was nothing but him in her heart and in her mind.

'He's had too many women in love with him!' Geertruida snapped, 'and you are just one of a crowd!'

'Do you think a man feels the same about every...woman he...loves?' Roxana asked.

'I would not be surprised,' Geertruida retorted.

But Roxana knew that she had asked a question it was impossible for her to answer.

Geertruida went away and Roxana suddenly found that while she was staring at her carving she could not see it for tears.

Could that kiss really have meant so little to him?

To her it had been a moment of divine light, a rapture that had lifted her soul into the skies, it had then become his and she had never been able to retrieve it again.

Because she could not carve with the tears

running down her cheeks she put down her chisel.

Knowing no-one could see her, she put her arms round the unfinished wood and laid her cheek against the Count's which she had already made smooth and very lifelike.

'I love...you!' she said beneath her breath. 'I love you and if I have to go on...suffering as I am...now...I think I shall...die!'

The tears ran down her face and were wet against the wood.

Then she knew she was not alone and looked up to find the Count staring at her!

CHAPTER SEVEN

For a moment they were both still as if turned to stone.

Then with a little cry like that of a child who finds safety after a frightening experience Roxana moved into the Count's arms.

He held her close against him, then he was kissing first her lips, then her wet eyes, the tears from her cheeks, and her lips again.

She felt as if her prayer had been answered. She had died and was in a Heaven so perfect, so wonderful that she was no longer breathing.

He kissed her until it was impossible to think but only to feel that he was there, that everything had changed, she was no longer alone or unhappy but a part of him as she had been before.

At last he raised his head to look down at her face radiant with a beauty he had never seen before, her eye-lashes wet, her lips trembling not with fear, but with the wonder of his kisses.

'I...love...you!' she murmured feeling as if her voice came from a long distance away.

'How could you have left me? How could you have gone away?' he asked. 'I have been frantic, off my head with terror in case I should never find you again!'

She gave a little sigh that was one of inexpressible happiness.

Then he was kissing her once again, holding her close against him as if he was afraid he might lose her for the second time, closer and closer until their bodies seemed to merge into each other's and their souls were one.

Finally when it seemed as if human nature must break under the strain he said in a voice that was curiously unsteady:

'I have found you, my lovely one, and I swear that I will never lose you another time. How soon will you marry me?'

He saw the light in her eyes as if a thousand candles had been lit inside her. Then she laid her head against his shoulder to say:

'What will the...Dutch say? How did you...get here without...their knowledge?'

As if the thought brought her fear for Karel back into her mind she gave a little cry of terror.

'They are not...with you? You have not... come to take...us back?'

'Of course not!' he said. 'Do you really think I would let you go back? It was clever of you, my darling, to escape. At the same time I wish you had trusted me.'

'How did you...find me? How...did you... get here?'

The questions seemed to tumble from her lips and he kissed her forehead before he said:

'It is quite a long story. Suppose we go and sit down somewhere comfortable? It is very hot and I would like one of Geertruida's cool drinks, if she will make me one.'

Roxana moved from his arms and took

his hand as she had done the night they had walked in the darkness through the forest.

At the same time she gave him a smile which was so radiantly happy, that he felt his heart turn over in his breast.

'Never,' he told himself, 'could any woman be so lovely, so exquisite in every way!'

They moved into an adjacent *balé* which was very like the one Roxana had used as a Sitting-Room in the North except that there was less furniture.

The most comfortable thing to sit on was a native bed which had been covered with a beautiful embroidered sarong in heavy silk.

Roxana left the Count for a moment and he heard her calling Geertruida, her voice seemed to vibrate with happiness and excitement.

A few seconds later she came back to him.

As she entered the *balé* she stood for a moment looking at him, then she ran towards him to say almost frantically:

'You are real! You are really here! I am

not...dreaming?'

'Have you dreamt of me often?' he asked in his deep voice.

'Every night...and when I have not been dreaming I have been...thinking of...you.'

'And crying for me?'

'I have...tried not to...do so.'

'Those tears are very precious,' he said and kissed her eyes.

They sat down on the makeshift sofa as if the intensity of their feeling had weakened them. Then looking up at him adoringly Roxana asked:

'Tell me how you found me.'

'You must thank Ida Anak Temu for that.'

'He told you?' Roxana exclaimed incredulously. 'I was sure he would keep my secret.'

'So he did, at first.'

'But how could you speak to him?'

'I took the Overseer of your village with me.'

'Of course...Tunas Kantor. He speaks several languages.'

'He speaks Dutch which was important from my point of view,' the Count said, 'and I shall always owe him a debt of gratitude.'

'Go on...tell me what happened,' Roxana prompted.

'Ponok had seen you go and, although he realised you did not wish to be seen he recognised the driver of your *gharry*.'

'He knew it was one of Ida Anak Temu's sons?' Roxana asked.

'He thought it was,' the Count replied. 'And so the Overseer and I went to the forest.'

He smiled before he went on:

'I promise you that your Master-carver was at first very discreet and disclaimed all knowledge of your whereabouts.'

'I knew he would be loyal,' Roxana murmured.

'But when I told him I was aware that it was his men who were moving your carvings and that it was his son who had taken you away he began to look a little uncomfortable.'

'You were not...unkind to him?'

'I would never be unkind to any friend of yours.'

'Then why did he tell you what you...wished to...know?'

'I told him I had to find you because I intended to marry you and I could not lose the only woman I had ever loved in my whole life.'

Roxana stared at him wide-eyed and he continued:

'The old man looked at me in the way that you told me he looks at a piece of wood, testing me, looking below the surface...'

'With his...soul!' Roxana whispered.

'Exactly!' the Count said, 'and that is what I knew he was doing and obviously, my darling, I passed the test!'

She pressed nearer to him as if she could not prevent herself and the Count's arm went round her.

'When he told me where you had gone and that I should find you safe in the house of his most famous pupil Gueda Tano, I was faced with a new problem.'

'How to...reach me?'

'I realised it was not going to be easy,' the Count said, 'first to get away from the Dutch and on no account to let them know where you were.'

'I have been...afraid,' Roxana confessed, 'terribly afraid that somehow they would find a way...of taking me...back.'

'I swear they will never do that,' the Count said. 'At the same time for your sake, my lovely one, I want no unpleasantness, especially from the Governor.'

Roxana blushed and hid her face against his shoulder.

'I felt...he was...menacing me.'

'That is something he will not do in the future,' the Count said firmly. 'At the same time I do not wish him to send unfavourable reports about you to Amsterdam.'

'Would he do that?' Roxana enquired.

'It is very unlikely,' the Count replied, 'because I have covered my tracks when I came here with what I thought was commendable ingenuity.'

'Tell me what you did.'

'Can you guess?'

She shook her head.

'No! How did you reach me?'

She thought as she spoke it must have been a very long ride and he could not have been lucky as she was in finding friends of Ida Anak Temu in every village.

'I came by sea,' the Count said.

'By sea?' Roxana exclaimed in astonishment.

'It seemed a sensible thing to do,' he said. 'I told the Governor that I intended to circle the island and see it from every aspect. He warned me very fervently against landing in the South as it was independent of the Dutch, and I said that in that case I would sail from Boulbeng in the North around the island to land at Lambok which is under Dutch protection.'

'And he approved of that idea?' Roxana enquired.

'I think quite frankly he was glad to be

rid of me. I interfered with his intensive search for you.'

'He did not...know where I had...gone?'

'When I left he was quite certain you were somewhere in the forest; but as there is a great deal of forest in the North I feel it will take him a considerable time to make sure that you are not hiding in some obscure village or even in a cave.'

Roxana put up her hands to hold onto him and he said:

'Once you are my wife, my darling, not all the Governors in the world shall frighten you. I will see to that!'

Roxana lifted her face to his, but before the Count could kiss her, Geertruida stepped onto the heightened floor with a tray in her hand.

On it was a long glass of fruit juice.

'Are you surprised to see me, Geertruida?' the Count enquired in Dutch.

'Yes, *Mijnheer!*'

'You do not sound very pleased,' the Count said accusingly. 'At the same time

I hoped that you would stay with us when we are married. My wife would not like to lose you after all you have been through together.'

'Married!'

There was no mistaking the expression in Geertruida's eyes.

As if the Count understood he said firmly:

'We are to be married, Geertruida, at the very first opportunity.'

'Thank God my prayers have been answered!' Geertruida exclaimed.

Then she turned hastily away because, as Roxana knew, she did not wish the Count to see the tears of thankfulness in her eyes.

'Geertruida was quite certain,' Roxana said when they were alone, 'that you were trifling with my affections!'

'I would never do that, my precious one,' he said. 'At the same time I will be honest and say I did not realise how desperately, frantically I loved you until you disappeared!'

He was still for a moment as if he was remembering the misery he had gone through, the fear that had made him panic-stricken at the thought that he would not find her again.

'I felt I was Prince Rama,' he said in a low voice, 'mad with despair, searching for his wife who was in the power of the demons.'

Roxana smiled.

'And you did not have Hanuman and his army of monkeys to help you.'

'I had Lalor who was a tower of strength,' the Count replied. 'He found me a good and serviceable boat manned by excellent seamen who brought me safely here.'

'It was such a clever idea,' Roxana said. 'When I wanted to get away from Bali I never thought of any ship except those which belonged to the Dutch.'

'We now have to find a steamer that will carry us to Singapore,' the Count said. 'They told me here at the Port that quite a number call on their way to the other islands.'

'It must not be a...Dutch ship,' Roxana said quickly.

'Are you still afraid?' the Count asked with a smile. 'The Dutch cannot hurt you when you are under my protection either as my wife or as my fiancée.'

'But...there is...Karel,' she said in a low voice. 'They might...still take Karel...away.'

'How could they do that?' the Count enquired.

'Because it is the law that orphans must be put in an Orphanage. They have several in Java.'

'Orphans?' the Count repeated in a puzzled voice.

Roxana looked at him, then she said:

'If you...believed me when I told you that Karel was...mine, I suppose...I thought... that Ida Anak Temu would have...told you the...truth.'

For a moment the Count was very still. Then he said:

'Karel is not—your child?'

'No, of course not!' Roxana answered. 'I only said that because I was so...frightened because you were...Dutch.'

'Then whose is he?'

The Count's voice sounded strange even to himself.

'He was Aunt Agnes's baby and she died soon after he was born.'

Roxana gave a little sigh at remembering the unhappiness of it, then she went on:

'She knew before we left Holland that she was having a baby after she and Pieter Helderik had been married for fifteen years. But she kept it a secret from him because she thought it would prevent him from coming to Bali.'

'Your—aunt's child!' The Count found it difficult to say the words.

'Are you saying,' Roxana asked in a very small voice, 'that you asked me to be your wife thinking that I had a...child though I was not...married?'

'Forgive me, my darling,' the Count replied. 'I should have trusted you. I should have known it was something you could never do, and yet the circumstantial evidence was against you.'

Roxana did not speak and he went on:

'The secrecy, the insinuations the Governor made, the fact that I found you asleep with the baby in your arms, and you told me...'

'Forgive me! Forgive me!' Roxana interrupted. 'You frightened me and I was... panic-stricken in case after all Geertruida and I had been...through to keep Karel hidden, he would be...taken away and...sent to an Orphanage.'

For a moment it was impossible for the Count to speak. He could only hold Roxana close against him, his lips against her hair.

Because he loved her in a way that he thought no man could ever have loved before, he had known that he was prepared to marry her whatever she had done in the past.

He had realised when he could not find her that the love they had for each other was too great, too perfect, to be concerned with anything but the fact that spiritually they were a part of each other and indivisible.

But now he found that Roxana was all he had thought her to be the first time he had kissed her: pure, innocent, everything he had longed for but thought it was impossible to find.

As if she understood what he was feeling Roxana said:

'To think you would have...married me believing such...things about me...all I can say is no man...could be so...wonderful, so...noble in...every way.'

She lifted her lips to his and for a moment he looked down into her eyes as if he could hardly believe she was real.

Then he was kissing her urgently, insistently, demandingly, and yet Roxana thought there was something else there too.

Perhaps a reverence, perhaps the idealism of a man who finds that his love is not only passionate and possessive but sacred.

★ ★ ★ ★

A long time later the Count said:

'We must make plans, my precious one. Let us go and talk to Gueda Tano and find out if he has any idea when there will be a ship in which we could travel to Singapore.'

Because she was so happy Roxana was prepared to do anything he asked.

She rose to her feet and the Count kissed her again before she fetched a sunshade to protect her from the burning rays of the sun.

They found Gueda Tano working at his carving in exactly the same way that the Count had seen Ida Anak Temu working at his.

Sitting cross-legged, he bowed his head when they appeared. He did not rise but commanded one of his apprentices to bring them chairs.

He was working on an intricate piece of exquisite carving which Roxana was sure was meant for one of the Temples.

What he had seen within a block of red hibiscus wood was a number of musicians and he was at the moment finishing off the figure of the flute-player.

As Roxana had found when she arrived, Gueda Tano unlike his teacher could not speak Dutch, because he hated the language, but he knew a little English.

Now he said to the Count with a smile that seemed to stretch from ear to ear:

'You find Mees Barclay *Mijnheer*? That good.'

'Yes, I have found her,' the Count said, 'and now we need your help.'

Gueda Tano made a gesture which indicated that he was at their service and the Count asked:

'Have you any idea when there will be a ship which can carry us to Singapore. I asked at the Port when I arrived and they said they did not think there would be one for perhaps two or three weeks.'

'That right,' Gueda Tano replied. 'One here three days ago. Now gone. Wait some time for other.'

'Then alternately,' the Count said, 'perhaps you could tell me if there is anyone in South Bali who could marry us?'

Roxana turned to look at him in astonishment and he said to her quietly:

'I cannot wait so long for you to be my wife, and what could be a more perfect place for a honeymoon?'

He was dazzled by the radiance in Roxana's face, then they looked pleadingly at the man sitting cross-legged beside them.

'You are Christians?' Gueda Tano enquired.

The Count nodded.

'No Christians in South Bali,' he said. 'English gone away. Dutch in North.'

He saw the disappointment on the Count's and Roxana's faces and asked:

'Why not Balinese marriage. You good people, our gods bless you. Mees Barclay great carver, like me.'

The Count looked at Roxana and he saw the question in her eyes.

Then as she did not speak he asked:

'Will you marry me here with the blessing of the gods in which we both believe?'

'C...could we...do that?'

'We can!' he answered, 'so long as you trust me to marry you again when we reach Singapore.'

'I...want to be...married to you.'

'As you will be,' he answered, 'by every law, book and vow that exists so that I can never lose you! But I do not want to wait.'

'Nor...do I,' Roxana whispered.

They did not have to tell Gueda Tano of their decision. He could see it in their faces and he said with a note of excitement in his voice:

'I arrange! Verry beautiful, verry good marriage. I speak with Priest.'

Roxana looked at the Count and her eyes were shining.

'I think it is the most perfect idea I have ever heard!' she said, 'to become your wife in "The Island of Paradise!" '

★ ★ ★ ★

A wedding is an excitement in every country and in every religion, but the Balinese had never had a wedding where the bride and bridegroom were from overseas and as Gueda Tano explained to the Count: 'Between two such handsome people.'

The Count however was aware that the reason the Priest was willing to perform the service even though they were not of his religion was that Roxana was blessed by the gods in having such great talent.

The people of Bali respected those who could carve because each in their own way were artists.

Roxana suspected that the very generous donation which the Count had offered to give the Temple had contributed also to the Priest's enthusiasm for such a ceremony.

But she had no wish to spoil the magical fairy-tale quality of the preparations by thinking of anything so mundane as money.

Gueda Tano, who was arranging everything, insisted that they must wait two days to give the women time to prepare the feast which was an important part of the ceremony.

'If we were really doing it properly,' Roxana said with a laugh, 'you would have to kidnap me first, which was traditional amongst the Balinese in the past.'

'What happened then?' the Count enquired.

'Although everyone knew that it would happen, the father was expected to be furious and to organise a rescue party. But it was arranged for them not to find the couple in their honeymoon hide-out.'

The Count looked puzzled and she laughed.

'A honeymoon in Bali always precedes the marriage.'

'A somewhat dangerous practice!' the Count said dryly, 'and I would not risk it where you are concerned.'

She smiled at him and he saw the love in her eyes and knew that he was blessed already by being the most fortunate man in the whole world.

'There is one other part of the wedding ceremonial which I am sure you will wish to skip,' Roxana said teasingly.

'What is that?'

'Just before the wedding there is an ancient initiation rite: if the bride or the bridegroom's teeth have not been filed it must be done before they are joined together as man and wife!'

'Good Heavens!' the Count exclaimed.

'It is part of Balinese Hinduism,' Roxana explained, 'and was performed so that the young people's souls would eventually be allowed to enter the Spirit World.'

'I refuse, refuse absolutely and categorically to have my teeth filed!' the Count declared.

'And so do I!' Roxana agreed. 'So let us hope we shall escape that part of the proceedings, at any rate!'

'You can be sure of that,' the Count replied, 'and anyway your teeth are perfect as they are.'

'Thank you,' Roxana said mockingly and he added more seriously:

'Just as I find everything about you is

perfect. One day I suppose there will be some flaws, but so far I have not found one.'

'Then please do not look too closely,' Roxana pleaded. 'I want to be...perfect and I pray every night that I shall be...worthy of...you.'

The Count gave an exclamation and drew her into his arms.

'How can you say such things to me?' he asked. 'The case is the exact opposite. I am not worthy of you. I have done so many things of which I am ashamed.'

He thought as he spoke of Luise van Heydberg and remembered how when he had thought he had lost Roxana he had been terrified in case this was the price he must pay for his misdeeds.

'The past is forgotten!' Roxana said softly. 'It is the future that...matters and I am your...future as you are...mine.'

'I ask for nothing else,' the Count replied.

They had lowered the bamboo wall so that as they talked together, they could not be seen from the court-yard.

'There is something I have to tell you,' Roxana said.

'What is it?'

'I did not tell the Dutch either here or in Holland who my father was.'

'And who is he?' the Count enquired. He did not appear very interested.

He was looking at Roxana's face as if every line of it delighted him and he knew he could never grow tired of watching the light in her eyes and the curve of her lips.

'When he was alive,' Roxana answered, 'Papa was leader of the House of Lords and Lord-in-Waiting to Queen Victoria.'

The Count smiled.

'I am very impressed, my darling, but I know that really your father was Jupiter and your mother Venus.'

He put his arms around her and his mouth took possession of hers so that everything ceased to be of any importance.

★ ★ ★ ★

When it was known they were to be married, there was ceaseless activity in the court-yard. All day the women were decorating it with *Lamaks.*

These were decorative strips made from a very young palm leaf. They were formally designed and interlaced so that the dark, pale and almost white green made intricate patterns.

The women pinned the designs with half-inch lengths of bamboo which was just as effective as metal pins.

It made the whole court-yard seem very festive and very beautiful, and everyone in the whole place kept bringing offerings of fruit, flowers, eggs, chickens and white rice on banana-leaf platters.

As more and more arrived every hour they became a crimson, emerald, blue, lime and white heap which grew into a glowing pyramid.

Roxana knew that in every kitchen in the village the men and women were working over sizzling, smoking food.

There were numerous sucking-pigs roasting on spits, which after the ceremony would be cut up and placed on banana leaves with beef or pork *satay* and large chunks of bacon fat on sticks.

It would be served with *penjon* or grated coconut hotly spiced with red and green chillis and *mritja* which was the Balinese word for Spanish pepper.

Although the Count was quite prepared to pay for anything that was wanted, there would, Roxana told him, be little drinking.

'The men like beer, rice-wine or palm-wine,' she said, 'but they are a most abstemious people and dislike drinking to excess, because for their minds to become fuddled is a sensation they despised.'

Because it was such a different marriage from anything she had ever imagined, it was in a way, she thought, more wonderful than any ordinary ceremony at home could have been.

It was part of the magic that she and the Count had felt for each other ever since they met, the magic they had found in the Ketjak and in that ecstatic moment when he had kissed her under the fragrant frangipani tree.

The Count had not stayed the two nights after his arrival as Roxana had expected him to do in her compound, although there was plenty of room because there were several empty *balés*.

Instead Gueda Tano had found him a house outside the village that had belonged at one time to an Englishman who had left a year ago and it had stayed empty ever since.

On Gueda Tano's instructions the village women had cleaned it and the Count's Valet had arranged everything for his master's comfort as he had been doing for many years when they had travelled together.

Geertruida had provided the Count with some of the linen sheets they had brought with them and, although Roxana had been too busy helping with the preparations in her own home to visit the Villa, she heard that he was very comfortable.

The Count had been able to purchase in one way or another anything that was missing.

It was typical, Roxana thought, that although the owner was unlikely to return, nothing had been stolen or removed from the villa.

She was quite sure that if the Count had not commandeered it for the weeks they had to wait for a ship, it would have remained just as it was.

Gradually the spiders, the birds, and later the bats would have taken up residence there and it would have crumbled into disrepair.

Knowing how attractive the guests at the wedding would look, with their flowers in their hair and their brilliant sarongs, Roxana was half-afraid they would eclipse her.

After a long discussion she finally decided to wear the prettiest of her white evening-gowns.

It was trimmed with lace on the bodice and swept round her slim body into a bustle of frill after frill of lace like a cascade down a hillside.

Geertruida made her a veil which fell on each side of her face to below her waist and there was a wreath of white flowers to halo her head.

She looked very lovely and at the same time ethereal, so that to the Count she was the very personification of Aphrodite.

He had sent her a bouquet of gardenias and as she waited for him to arrive she thought nothing could be more perfect than that they should be married not only with the blessing of the Pedanda but among the simple, affectionate people she loved.

There would be none of the criticism, the jealousy, or the pomposity that would have undoubtedly been present at their wedding in either England or Holland.

'He's here!' Geertruida exclaimed excitedly as the Count walked into the *balé* where Roxana was waiting, hidden from the crowds by the bamboo blind.

For a moment he just stood looking at

her and she could see nothing but love in his eyes and an expression on his face that she knew instinctively no woman had ever seen before.

He walked across to her and without touching her said:

'This is a very strange wedding, my lovely darling, but I believe that the ancient gods will bless their own. You look like a goddess and I worship you with my heart, my mind and my soul.'

Roxana knew as he spoke that he was repeating a vow that was as sacred as any he could have made in front of the altar of St Paul's Cathedral.

She looked up at him and said very softly:

'I love you...and there is...nothing else in the...whole world but...you!'

He gave her his arm, and dramatically Geertruida pulled up the bamboo screen which hid them from the people outside and they walked into the court-yard.

It was packed with those who had been waiting almost since first light.

The men all had scarlet hibiscus behind their ears, the women wore garlands of flowers over their naked breasts and had white gardenias and frangipani blossoms in their hair.

The Priest was standing behind a *lamak* draped shrine. He wore a dark green sarong and white *baju*, the cap of his office, and before him on a carved box was a brass bell, flowers and containers of holy water.

Gueda Tano had already told Roxana and the Count what they were to do and they sat down on their heels facing the Priest.

The Count held out an offering of fruit on a palm-leaf which represented all the other offerings.

The Priest dedicated it by touching his bell, praying silently, breaking off a piece of leaf and flicking it with drops of holy water.

Then he snapped a white string, cast one piece away and threw after it some buds of gardenia which had lain in front of him.

After that for some minutes only the Priest moved.

He sat with his eyes closed, praying, making rhythmic gestures with his hands over the flowers and towards the bride and bridegroom.

In the background the silver and gold notes of the gamelan orchestra played music which might have come from the movement of the green rice fields or the leaves of the frangipani tree blowing in the breeze.

There was absolute silence among those watching and Roxana prayed in her heart that she might bring the Count happiness, and that they would love each other until the end of their lives.

At last the Priest rose and taking a bowl of holy water he sprinkled drops of it with his long fingers on Roxana's head, then on the Count's.

Then he handed them both a Tjempaka blossom. The Count put it in his button-hole—a Balinese bridegroom would have put it behind his ear—and Roxana fixed hers in her hair.

The Priest then gave Roxana a square of palm leaf and the Count was handed a jewel-handled *kris* which was the traditional sword that all Balinese carried into battle.

He pierced the leaf and knew that this had a sacred meaning that was apparent. But he realised Roxana did not understand and adored her for her innocence.

Finally the Priest handed them both eggs which were symbols of fertility, which they passed backwards and forwards to each other as he rang his brass bell.

Then he raised his arms to the gods above and called in a loud voice for their blessing.

Roxana looked at the Count, saw the expression in his eyes and prayed:

'Please God, let me give him sons as strong and as handsome as he is.'

Then as if she realised he could read her thoughts, the colour rose in her cheeks and the Count knew that she was as pure in mind and body as he had always wanted his wife to be.

Love surged through his body like a live flame as her hand touched his.

For Roxana they were both transfigured by the ecstasy and glory of the gods, the sunlight encircled them and they were one with the Divine...

★ ★ ★ ★

The music played more loudly, the ceremony was over, the children began to laugh and run about.

Geertruida, carrying Karel in her arms, was talking to a number of Balinese mothers, although they could not understand anything each other was saying.

Cups of Balinese beer made from dried rice was handed round and the feast began.

The children waited with hungry eyes for *lawar* platters of raw meat chopped fine and mixed with spiced coconut.

The Count and Roxana thanked the Priest and Gueda Tano and kissed Karel. Then taking Roxana by the hand the Count drew her away from the excited, laughing people in the court-yard and out through the gate-way.

'Where are we going?' she asked.

He smiled and helped her into a painted and decorated *gharry* which was draped with garlands of flowers.

Only a few people realised they were leaving and hurried from the court-yard to wave to them as the *gharry* drove off.

The Count pressed Roxana's hand against his lips.

'Do you feel that you are really my wife?' he asked.

Her eyes were like stars as she answered:

'It was such a beautiful ceremony, and I know that I bear your name and we are man and wife on the island of Bali.'

'I intend to marry you in Singapore and also, if you wish, in India and wherever else we stay before we arrive home!'

'It is what *you* wish,' Roxana said softly. 'Now I have no more decisions to make, for you will make them for me.'

The Count put his arm around her and they drove in silence.

The road came to an end and there was only a path winding under the trees until in front of her she saw the house where he had been staying.

Inevitably it was surrounded with a wide verandah but the flowering shrubs unchecked had grown in such profusion that they had encircled it, climbed up the pillars and over the roof.

The whole villa was nothing but a bouquet of brilliant coloured flowers.

Roxana gave a cry of sheer delight.

'It is like a house in a fairy-story!'

'That is what I thought,' the Count said, 'and why, my fairy-tale bride, I brought you here.'

The *gharry* stopped. The driver wished them "Good luck!" and drove away grinning.

'Our first home,' the Count said softly and picked Roxana up in his arms.

He carried her across the threshold and

into the house.

The Sitting-Room was small but airy with white walls, and everywhere there were flowers.

There were great banks of gardenias and lilies in every corner scenting the atmosphere with a fragrance that was almost overpowering.

Through an open door she could see a Bed-room. It also was white with a big carved bed draped like sails of a ship. It looked out on the flower-filled verandah to where in the distance there was the vivid blue of the sunlit sea.

Roxana turned towards the Count and asked:

'Does it please you, my precious one?'

'It is so beautiful! Could any place in the world offer a more perfect background for our love?'

'Nowhere!' he said firmly. 'I love you, my darling, in a way for which I have no words and therefore I can only express it as I did before.'

He pulled her towards him and Roxana thought that of all the kisses he had given her this was more wonderful, more poignant, because now she was his wife and nothing could ever separate them again.

'I love you!' she tried to say but the Count was right. There was no need for words.

It was there in the closeness of their bodies, in their minds and in their hearts.

It was in the scent of the flowers, the beauty of the little house and in the island itself, enveloping and protecting them, keeping them safe and together for all time.

It was all so rapturous and so divine that when the Count raised his head Roxana made a little murmur, because she could not bear to lose, even for one moment, the rapture he evoked in her.

He took his arms away, then lifting her left hand drew a gold wedding ring from his waist-pocket.

He kissed it.

Then he said very quietly:

'With this ring I thee wed, with my body

I thee worship, for all eternity my lovely wife, and beyond.'

He put the ring on her finger and kissed it.

As the tears came into her eyes from sheer happiness he drew Roxana into the Bedroom and took first the wreath from her head and then her veil.

He looked at her for a moment then gently pulled pins from her hair so it fell over her shoulders.

She was trembling with excitement she had never known before as he took her once again into his arms.

'You are mine,' he said. 'Mine, my adorable, perfect little wife. Tell me that you love me too.'

His lips were very close to hers and she whispered against them:

'I love you, my wonderful...husband, and...we are...lovers...in Paradise.'

The publishers hope that this book has given you enjoyable reading. Large Print Books are especially designed to be as easy to see and hold as possible. If you wish a complete list of our books, please ask at your local library or write directly to: Magna Print Books, Long Preston, North Yorkshire, BD23 4ND England.